I0565489

FIRST (99 DADDIES BOOK 1)

CASEY COX

Copyright © 2020 Casey Cox. All rights reserved.

ISBN: 978-0-6489983-0-3

This book is a work of fiction, as well as a more than suitable answer to the question - things that make you go hmmmm? Any references to real people, organizations, foot stools, ice cream flavors, locations and TV shows are simply intended to offer a semblance of reality and are completely fictitious. Characters, names, plot points and dialogue are figments of the author's imagination. Is that a little scary? Perhaps.

The gorgeous cover is courtesy of the wonderful Cate Ashwood. The gorgeous lack of errors, typos and misspellings is due to Louisa, Lori, Katie and my wonderful and dedicated Advance team. (Special shout out to Leslie Copeland. You have no idea how your words of support and encouragement helped me to keep going to create a story I hope readers will find entertaining, heartwarming, interesting and yes...gorgeous.)

No part of this book may be reproduced in any form or by any electronic or mechanical means, including information storage and retrieval systems, without written permission from the author, except for the use of brief quotations in a book review. It is also recommended to not read this book while showering.

SYNOPSIS

First: (adverb)
a: before another in time, space, or importance
b: for the first time.
See also: Stirling "First-Time Daddy" Bishop.

A boy who can't find what he wants.
A Daddy who doesn't know what he needs.

With his big blue eyes, lean frame, and propensity for adorkable clumsiness, Mikey Harrison is a Daddy magnet...for the wrong type of Daddy. Those who mistake his desire to serve as an open invitation to mistreat him and abuse his trust.

But all of that changes when he lays his eyes on Stirling Bishop. Sure, the strong, silent (and irresistibly sexy) type ticks all of his boxes, but it's the tenderness underlying Stirling's strength that makes him achingly irresistible.

For Mikey, it's insta-love.

For Stirling, it's insta-huh?

Despite looking like he was put on this earth to be the Daddy of every boy's dreams, the thought of dating a younger guy has never even crossed Stirling's mind, much less the idea of being a Daddy.

But there's no denying that Mikey awakens something deep within him—the desire to dominate, the need to care. It's been dormant, yet bubbling under the surface within him for his entire life.

Can Mikey help Stirling find the strength he needs to be the Daddy he was meant to be...and become the Daddy of Mikey's dreams?

FIRST
First is a Daddy/boy, May-December gay romance featuring a strong, silent, first-time Daddy, and an eager boy who can show him the way. Come along for the ride and enjoy some crazy/sexy/cool shenanigans including: impromptu foot rubs, naked butlers, a crew of sassy friends, lots of LOLs, and all the feels on the way to a heartwarming HEA.

First is the first book in the *99 Daddies* series. Each book in the series will contain overlapping characters and storylines, so you may enjoy them more by reading them in order.

99 DADDIES
99 Daddies is a hilarious, entertaining, and heartwarming Daddy/boy, May-December MM romance series.

Escape to Daylesford, the (fictional) Daddy capital of America.

If you love steamy and complex Daddy/boy dynamics, May-December gay romances with a twist, sweet and sassy MM age-gap romances—and chasing those guaranteed HEAs—you'll love it here.

So come along and meet the 99 Daddies of Daylesford. Who will be YOUR favorite?

CHAPTER ONE

MIKEY

"What if I have to sneeze...?"

A thick eyebrow shot up in my direction.

"Or go to the bathroom...?"

Side-eye. The curious, not the bitchy kind.

"Or what if it starts to hurt and I need to move? I mean, this tray is so heavy..."

Nick's lips tugged upward in the faintest hint of a smile.

"If you need to move for whatever reason, just tell me. I'll call someone over to help us out." He turned to look at me. His brown eyes friendly and his voice gentle, reassuring as always. "In the meantime, Mikey, just stick to the brief, okay? Smile and stay still."

Ladies and gentlemen, Nicholas Macklin. The voice of reason, my personal protector, and best friend since junior high.

Also the person responsible for me being on my hands and knees, naked except for a pair of flesh-colored briefs with a heavy eight-foot-long silver platter of food on my back. Well, technically it was spread across both of our backs.

Nick was on his hands and knees right beside me, as he always was whenever he roped me into whatever crazy shenanigans he was up to. At least this crazy shenanigan paid well and kept us out of trouble. For the most part.

You see, we were naked butlers which was kind of like being a waiter minus the clothes, combined with a stripper minus the dancing. We showed up and entertained guests at parties, serving food and drinks, wearing only tiny—*tiny*—aprons around our waists, bowties, and massive smiles. Class...with ass.

It sounded sketchy when Nick first told me about it a year ago, but there was a strict no-touch policy which our boss—the big and burly bear of a man, Hunter Greyson—was incredibly strict about enforcing.

He didn't tolerate shit from anyone and made sure we were all clear on our roles. We were entertainers, not sex workers. Flirting was fine, fingers in assholes were not. You wouldn't believe how many times people tried *that*.

All in all, it was actually a pretty good gig, and I enjoyed it. I got paid to be eye candy and to serve food and drinks to men at parties and events all around town. I had no problem with men looking at me, and I certainly had no problem with *serving* men, either.

Tonight's party was a deviation from the usual brief. Instead of walking around with platters of food and drinks, we were human furniture. It was the very specific request of the party host, an attractive Daddy by the name of Porter Jones.

We were in his sunken living room, in his super-fancy house, in one of Daylesford's nicest tree-lined streets. It was his friend's fortieth and he wanted to do something memorable. So two butlers were on serving duty, while Nick and I were human furniture.

Hence the heavy, eight-foot silver tray across both of our backs.

Hence me having to stay still. If I moved and tipped the tray over, it would most likely cover my aforementioned best friend in all sorts of party snacks, chips, and dips. Said best friend would not be very happy about that.

The tray was heavy, like really heavy, and already starting to strain my back. I grimaced, fighting against the urge to readjust my hands and knees. I must have moved a little, though, because Nick shot me his *what-are-you-doing?* look.

"Stay still, Mikey."

"Sorry, I'm trying," I replied. I *was* trying. But standing still wasn't easy for me. I was a kinda clumsy, fidgety kid growing up, who had morphed into a kinda clumsy, fidgety twenty-four-year-old kinda, sorta adult.

And being quiet? Yeah, not my thing at all. My mind was always racing with a constant stream of thoughts and ideas, with my mouth following closely behind. Most people had a filter between their brain and their mouth. I didn't. Or if I did, mine was permanently broken.

I looked down at the floor, taking a deep breath to steady myself and adjust to the cold, heavy tray on my back. Then I looked farther down my body at what we were wearing.

Given our slightly unusual assignment for the evening, Hunter had insisted that we wear flesh-colored briefs instead of our usual waist aprons, in order to prevent wayward fingers from going places they shouldn't.

We'd also skipped the bow ties, because furniture doesn't wear a bow tie. That's some naked butler 101 logic for you right there. You're welcome.

In front of us, a pretty typical party scene was playing out. There were balloons and streamers everywhere, nineties R&B

music was playing in the background, and a smattering of Daddies and boys were mingling and having a good time.

"Incoming," Nick said. I stiffened my body as a guy wearing a crisp, navy blue linen shirt and sporting a wide smile approached.

"Well look at you, big boy." He gave me a cursory look up and down, but it was Nick who he was speaking to.

"See anything you like, handsome?" Nick shot back, flashing a devilishly sexy smile, not missing a beat.

The guy knelt down and looked over the platter we were holding up on our backs. He picked up a couple of strawberries.

"These will have to do...for now," he said.

"Well if you want something sweeter, you know where to find me," Nick replied cheekily.

The guy pored over Nick's body, soaking it all in. Nick preened, turning his face upward, and smiled. He loved getting attention. The guy slipped a note into Nick's briefs and Nick pouted his lips into a kiss before the guy turned to walk away.

"He was cute," I said, once the guy was out of earshot.

"Yeah, he was okay. Not really my type though."

It never ceased to amaze me how confident Nick was. He could turn his flirting game on like a light switch. My flirting switch was a bit like my brain filter. Permanently broken.

He'd been that way since junior high. Ever since Brett Evlin walked up to us in eighth grade gym class and gave us the nickname, *the fatty and the fag*. Nick, being Nick, fought back. With words, and fists when needed.

Me being me, I ran away from the bullying, the taunts, the cruel nicknames. I scampered away into the corner, learning to hide who I was and what I really wanted.

That went for being gay, but it also went for being a boy, a submissive type of boy, who wanted nothing more than to please.

To serve. Desires I had suppressed deep inside of me all of my life, but desires that refused to disappear nonetheless.

I loved Nick's I-don't-give-a-shit attitude, and I was still optimistically waiting for the day when some of it would begin to rub off on me.

"A bit too young for me," Nick continued, by way of explanation.

"Ah, still going through your Daddy phase, I see," I teased.

Nick's thick eyebrows arched up.

"Oh please, as if you can talk. Mikey Harrison, aka Daylesford's biggest Daddy magnet. And don't even pretend for a minute you don't know what I'm talking about."

If his hands were free, I would have had his fingers wagging in my face right about now.

I pursed my lips into a thin line. I hated it when he was right.

I guess technically we were both boys, but Nick was...a big boy. *Thicc* wasn't just a word emblazoned on his favorite midriff-baring tank top, it described his body to a tee—massive biceps, a plump, round ass and a soft, big belly. A combination that brought all the boys to his yard.

While Nick was unconventional in his twinkness, I was about as typical as they came. Tall and slender, with blue eyes and a baby face that made me look a lot younger than twenty-four.

Until recently, I had bright blond hair. But after a bad breakup with the granddaddy of Daddy assholes, I decided I needed a change. A bottle of black hair dye seemed to be the perfect solution.

I thought it might turn some clients off, given it was such a sharp look, but if anything, it seemed to have had the opposite effect. I was making more in tips now with a thick mop of black hair than I ever did as a blond.

Which was a good thing, because when you're a naked

butler, the math is really quite simple: good looks plus a little friendly flirting equals great tips.

"How often is *you-know-who* texting you these days?" Nick asked, his lips tightly pursed, deliberately avoiding saying the name. I did know who. My asshole ex, Brian.

I let out a loud sigh. "Mainly just abusive texts when he drinks."

"So, every day, then?"

I chuckled. He wasn't far off. Brian had hurt me really badly. We had been together for almost a year, and had broken up three months earlier.

It hadn't been a good relationship from the start, but I'd ignored my feelings and pushed through anyway, only seeing what I wanted to see, glossing over the bad stuff. In other words, typical me.

I learned a good lesson from that relationship. There are two types of Daddies: the good ones, who understand the proper way to treat a boy, and the bad ones, who twist and misuse the control and trust placed in them.

Nick was right. I was a Daddy magnet...for the wrong type of Daddy.

"Yeah, well, I'm over men," I announced.

The words sounded even more pathetic when I heard them out loud than they did in my head. I held back a wince, which I hoped he couldn't see.

"Really?" Nick asked, barely able to contain his *I-don't-believe-you* chuckle. "Look around, Mikey. Are you telling me there is no one at this party you would fuck?"

Hmm...I glanced around the party in front of us. There were a few younger guys, but they were outnumbered by the beary-looking Daddy types. Strong, older men with experience etched into the lines of their chiselled faces. Solid men with muscles and bodies that were made to be held on to.

Just my type.

Normally.

When I wasn't announcing that I was over men.

I narrowed my eyes, looking a little harder around the room. The tiniest of tiny glimmers of hope filled my chest as I looked around at the men, a barely audible voice within me hoping that maybe he was here, my ultimate someone. The Daddy that was just right for me. I swallowed down hard, pushing that voice back down.

"Nope, no one," I answered glumly once I'd had a proper look.

"Do you know what the green dip is?" a British-sounding voice to my right asked. I hadn't even noticed the guy walk up to us.

I turned and looked up.

"I'm not sure," I said, plastering a wide smile onto my face. "Probably guacamole?"

"Oh right, yes, thank you," the voice replied, and before I could get a proper look at him, he had turned around and begun walking away.

"God, I hate British accents," I whispered to Nick.

Brian was from the UK, and his accent made him sound like the pompous asshole he was. Damn him, he'd ruined British accents for me.

"Really? I think they're hot," Nick replied. "Remember that English guy I was dating last summer?"

"Dating...for the weekend?" I said with a smile. "Yeah, I remember."

"Smart ass," Nick said, before continuing. "I loved his dirty talk in bed. He kept saying *fuck me, fuck me*, but with his accent it came out as *fook-mi, fook-mi*. I kept thinking to myself, what the hell's a *fook-mi*? I thought it was like a Japanese headscarf or something...So hot."

His brown eyes were shining brightly, and he was practically drooling at the memory.

"Why? You got a thing for Japanese headscarves or something?" I teased.

"No, I've got a thing for hot British guys who want me to *fook* them."

I started to laugh, which made the tray wobble against my back. Nick shot me a pointed look and I steadied myself.

But I could feel a restlessness starting to rise within me. It felt like we had been here all night already and I wanted to get up and move. My mind, racing with thoughts of asshole British exes and a Daddyless future, wasn't helping.

Was I over men? Could I be, when I knew just how much I needed the connection I could only ever feel when I was my truest self?

A boy.

A boy who would do anything to please his Daddy. To make him smile. To make him know how special and wonderful he was. To make him feel like the true, strong man that he was. To get him rock hard and make him come harder than he'd ever come in his life.

These urges tore through me, they were a part of me. They filled something within me, something so deep and so primal that even I didn't fully understand it.

Nick started talking about a guy he had met at a party the previous weekend as I let my eyes wander back around the room. I wasn't looking at anything, or anyone, in particular. My mind was still filled with thoughts of Brian.

Stupid, sexy, British, bar-owning Brian. Someone I had put so much love and trust and faith into, only to have it all thrown back in my face in the worst possible way. I bit down and braced myself against the flood of memories wanting to come back. I couldn't let them.

I had to stay still.

Nick was still happily talking away to himself, and I was still happily pretending to listen. My gaze was suddenly drawn to three men standing at the top of a small staircase that led into the sunken living room we were in.

They were all classic Daddy types, in their late thirties, maybe early forties. Muscular and masculine, with broad shoulders and distinct, attractive faces. They were well-dressed and tall, all six-foot-something, but the man standing on the left hovered a good four inches above the other two.

The men were joking and laughing, clearly good friends. Suddenly, another man approached and joined them. He was greeted with a series of hugs from each of the men.

In some ways, he looked just like them. Same age, tall, short brown hair, and wearing a tight-fitting black t-shirt that perfectly showed off his massive biceps and narrowed down nicely, hugging into his tight waist. I barely even realized my tongue was dragging over my bottom lip.

But there was something else about him that caught my eye. I could see it in the way he moved. There was a deliberate sturdiness in how he carried himself, that sent a warmth to the center of my chest...and an electric jolt of desire straight to the head of my cock.

I looked down and saw the growing hardness forming in my flesh-colored briefs. I didn't care. I just had to be still, no one had said anything about not getting hard.

I looked back up and squinted, desperate to see the details of the man's face, but he was standing too far away. There was a whole party between us.

Damn, I wanted him nearer. I wanted to see his face close up, to hear how deep his voice was, to know what kind of scent he had.

I wanted to see him.

The men around him were talking and laughing loudly, but for some reason, he wasn't. He would smile every once in a while, though, and what a fucking amazing smile it was when he did. It lit up the whole room between us and pulled me in. My heart started thumping harder in my chest.

I needed to see him.

But he was holding back. What was going on with him? What was happening underneath that hard-bodied, perfectly sculpted exterior? I had no way of knowing, but I could tell he was the strong and silent type.

Exactly my type.

"Hey, Mikey, are you even listening to me? Hello...? Earth to Mikey."

"Sorry, what?" I breathed, not moving my head, unable to take my eyes off the irresistible man on the other side of the room.

The strong and silent guy. The kind of guy that talked with his eyes, more than his mouth. The big, burly Daddy with the massive arms that were made to wrap around somebody's body. Ideally mine.

"Who are you looking at?" Nick asked as he tried to follow my gaze, but there were too many people between me and the Daddy of my fucking dreams. Way too many people. "The guy in the lumberjack hoodie standing by the door?" he guessed.

"No," I said, my eyes still glued to the gorgeous man. "Him, by the stairs. The guy in the black shirt."

My words came out as breathless pants.

"Oh...yeah. He's nice," Nick said as his face lit up. "Actually, they're all kinda nice," he added, stating the blatantly obvious as he took in all four men. "Look at that hot silver fox standing in the middle. Mmm, mmm, mmm. I could gobble him up for dinner and give him a dessert he'd never forget."

I ignored the lip smacking coming from Nick's direction.

"Now that right there Nicholas, is the Daddy of my dreams. He is fucking perfect," I said, finally peeling my eyes off the man and turning to look at Nick.

Just the thought of him made me weak. A shiver torpedoed up my spine, causing the tray on our backs to shake.

"Whoa there, horsey," Nick said, trying to calm me down. "If I end up covered in strawberries and guacamole because of you, you are going to pay."

"Sorry," I said, clearing my throat and trying to steady myself, pushing aside all the sexy thoughts about a certain sexy Daddy doing all sorts of sexy things to me.

"Besides," Nick said as his lips descended into that all-too-familiar shit-eating grin of his. "I thought you were over men?"

God, I wished I could give him the finger.

Or see him covered in strawberries and guacamole.

CHAPTER TWO

STIRLING

Just before I opened the heavy wood-paneled front door to let myself into Porter's house, I stopped, forcing a smile. It stretched my face in a weirdly tight way, but it looked better. I may have been grumpy, tired, and late, but I didn't want to ruin everyone's night. Again.

It was my best friend Steel Crawford's birthday. His fortieth, no less. The guy had done so much for me. I didn't know how I would have survived the court case and the last three years without him.

I walked in and saw my three closest friends huddled at the top of the stairs. My jaw loosened and the smile eased into a genuine one at the sight. Steel was standing in the middle, flanked by Porter and Hudson on either side.

We had become good friends while attending the University of Daylesford. Twenty years later, we were as close as ever. The original quad squad. We were all turning forty that year, with Steel kicking things off.

"Gentlemen," I said as I reached them.

"Where?" Porter said, snapping his head around, his light green eyes darting around the room. "Oh, you mean us." He smiled as he leaned in for a hug.

He was the "Samantha" of the group, nicknamed after the *Sex and the City* character. Let's just say he had a high sex drive and no qualms about sharing every explicit detail of his sexual adventures with us. He was also the chief of staff to the mayor of Daylesford, but we all knew that was just a stepping stone. The man had his eyes set firmly on the top job. Not that he'd ever admit it, of course. That was the one thing he didn't like talking about.

Birthday boy Steel greeted me with his usual tight bear squeeze. He pulled me in close and said, "Thanks for coming. I know how tired you are."

He wore a pair of tight blue jeans that looked like they'd been painted on, and his favorite Incubus shirt that he'd bought when we saw them play at Daylesford Arena almost a decade ago.

He'd run some gel through his stylish silver mane and had a thick leather bracelet covering his left wrist. He looked more like a rock star than a lawyer—one that ran his own firm, no less. The man made forty look damn good.

A pang of guilt pummelled my stomach as I pulled away from him. Was I that obvious? Clearly I was, and I hated it. He was my best friend. I didn't want to be a downer on his big night.

I looked him straight in the eye, stretched out my lips again, and said, "Hey, I wouldn't miss this for the world. Happy birthday, my friend."

His face lit up with a wide smile and the heavy feeling in my stomach lifted a little. This was his night, and I was determined to be here for it. I'd have plenty of time to be grumpy and tired later.

Last up was Hudson the Great, pulling me in to his massive six-foot-six frame. The dude was a beast, a walking wall of muscle. With his imposing size, shaved head, bright and intricate tattoos covering every square inch of skin on both arms, and his low, deep voice, Hudson seemed like one scary dude. But really, he was a gentle giant.

"Good to see you, man," he said in that low, yet friendly rumble of his.

"You too, buddy," I said.

"So, Porter, care to fill us in on what we're seeing here?" Steel said. I looked around the party, which was taking place in Porter's sunken living room, with some of it spilling over a little into the adjoining formal dining room.

It looked pretty normal from what I could see. There was some music playing, but it wasn't offensively loud. There was a big *Happy Birthday* sign hung on the far wall, along with balloons and streamers scattered around the room. A decent-sized crowd had shown up, and everyone seemed happy, chatting and laughing away. All the trappings of a normal birthday party, really.

Then I spotted a shirtless guy walking around holding a tray with drinks on it. Then another shirtless guy, walking around with a tray of hors d'oeuvres. Then I looked down and noticed that the men weren't just shirtless, they were pantless too.

They each wore a tiny apron around their waists that covered their fronts, but left their asses exposed, which helped explain why so many whiplash-inducing head spins followed the men wherever they went. Naked guys walking around the party? Clearly, this was all Porter's idea.

"Hey, you only turn forty once," Porter replied, raising his hands all innocent-like and smiling widely. "Might as well make it memorable, right? Besides, I don't hear anyone complaining."

A round of chuckles followed.

"And don't worry, my friend," he said in my direction. "I've thought of you too."

"What does that mean?" I asked, not entirely sure I wanted him to answer.

"Oh, you'll see. The night is still young."

I grumbled under my breath but said nothing else.

Porter began one of his long and intricately detailed sexcapade stories. As I looked at the guys, my three closest friends in the world, I couldn't help but feel a knot in my stomach. I was the black sheep of the group. The loser black sheep. They were all successful and living their best lives.

I wasn't. I was stuck, my life caught up in a neverending court case that was consuming all of my time, energy, and money. Sure, I still had my construction business, but that was requiring sixty-hour weeks from me, on a good week.

The last three years had been brutal, ever since my mom died. As if losing her wasn't painful enough, how she passed away ended up being just as traumatic.

It was neglect, pure and simple. The retirement community where she'd lived with my father failed in their duty of care. At least, that was what Steel and I had been trying to prove in court for the last three years. Three fucking years.

It was exhausting and draining. It left me grumpy, tired, and...single.

Well, my ex, Richard, and his inability to keep his dick in his pants was what had left me single. I'd decided to surprise him one day about ten months ago. I knew he had the afternoon off, so I thought we could spend some time together, some surprise quality time.

It was me who got the surprise though.

From the moment I stepped into our house, I was assaulted by the unmistakable sounds of sex filling the air. My head instantly knew what was happening, but for some reason, my heart needed to see it.

As I made my way down the hallway, the grunts and moans —some familiar and others not—got louder, rougher. I inched closer, reaching the bedroom door that had been left open. With my heart thumping against my chest, I peeked inside the bedroom. Our bedroom.

There he was. Richard, my Richard, thrusting balls deep into some guy lying on his back, his legs spread wide, flailing about with each thrust. Their combined greedy, urgent sounds filled the room as the bed rocked back and forth. Our bed.

It's funny how you never really know somebody until you break up with them. Despite having been a generally good guy— fucking whats-his-name in our bed aside—our breakup brought out the worst side of Richard. His greed and nastiness rose to the surface. Manipulation too. He tried to convince me it was my fault he'd cheated because *I wasn't there for him in that way* anymore.

He ended up taking half of what wasn't his—my house and my 401K—but at least not my construction business. My livelihood. My escape. My sixty-hour-a-week escape.

"So how does it feel to be entering your first official year of Daddyhood?" Hudson ribbed Steel gently.

"Gimme a break, man," Steel protested as he waved over one of the shirtless, pantless servers who was carrying a tray of what looked like bright green jello shots. "I've been a Daddy for years. Being a Daddy is a state of mind, not a number."

He carefully picked up four shots and handed them to us, saving one for himself.

"To Steel," Porter said.

We all raised our glasses into the air.

"To Steel," we said in unison.

The lethal-tasting concoction ignited the back of my throat.

A warm feeling filled my chest as I looked at my friends, their faces soured from the drink. We'd shared a lot over the last twenty years, but one big difference was that all three of them were Daddies, and I was not.

They had all been into younger guys for at least the last five years, Steel probably for a bit longer than that. They were Daddies, Porter was also a Dom, and they were all very active in the lifestyle. Each of them was a member at Revolver, Dayleford's premier BDSM club.

Not that I had ever been there. I had no problem with that. With any of it. At all. It was just that, for me, younger guys seemed, I don't know...immature. They didn't know what they wanted. They hadn't lived yet.

Although, who the fuck was I to talk? My life wasn't exactly going all that great at the moment. Maybe dating a younger guy wouldn't be such a bad thing?

Talking never came naturally to me. But I was happy being quiet because it gave me time to think and process. When I did talk, I said what I meant and meant what I said. But just because I didn't share every last graphic detail of my sex life like Porter, didn't mean I was as vanilla as I had led the guys to believe.

Heck, I wasn't even as vanilla as I tried to make myself believe. It's amazing what you can suppress, how deeply you can push your desires away, almost to the point where they disappear. Almost.

Not that I had been getting much action anyway. Between my business and the court case, my sex life had been reduced to rubbing one out in the shower every few days, when I wasn't too tired and could actually be bothered to get it up. God, that sounded pathetic.

That *was* pathetic.

"And what about you, Mr. Bishop?" Steel said.

Porter must have finally wound his story up, judging by the wide-eyed look of shock written across Hudson's face. The big man shakily reached for his drink.

"What do you mean *what about me*?" I asked, suddenly very aware of three sets of eyes on me.

"When's the last time you got laid?"

We all knew the answer to that question. Not since Richard.

"I...uh..." Heat creeped up my neck.

"I mean, look around, you've got your pick of some of Daylesford's finest boys right here," Steel continued.

"You guys know I'm not into younger guys," I said, lifting my drink to my lips.

Although Richard had been my age, and look at how that had turned out.

"There are some older men here too, if you prefer," Hudson added gently.

I forced a smile and looked out at the party. There were a lot of good-looking guys. But in all honesty, starting a relationship was the last thing on my mind. I would just have to be content with being grumpy, tired, and horny.

Thankfully, the guys didn't push any further and went back to talking, their gentle ribbing fading into the background as I looked around the party again. I suppressed a yawn.

"How are you holding up, buddy?" I heard Steel's deep voice as he placed his arm around my shoulder protectively.

"I'm good, thanks," I said as a yawn finally escaped from my mouth.

Damn it. It was my best friend's birthday and here I was, yawning like some old grandpa.

"You look tired, my friend." It was an observation, not a judgement. "Thank you for coming. I know you've got a lot going on and I really appreciate you being here tonight."

"Hey, there was no way I was going to miss my best friend turning forty. I'm sorry for being such a downer."

"No need to apologize, man. In fact, Porter and I have got you covered."

There was a cheeky gleam in his eye. I knew that look. That naughty *let's fuck some shit up* look that had gotten us into bucketloads of trouble in college.

"We had a feeling you might be tired, so..."

His voice trailed off as he grabbed my hand and shot Porter a devilish grin over his shoulder. Before I could say or ask anything, I was being dragged down the stairs and across the crowded floor. We walked through the middle of the room toward the far corner.

"You look tired," he said again, more loudly than normal and in an odd, over-the-top kind of way. I eyed him suspiciously. What was he up to? "Why don't you put your feet up?" he said, leaning over to pick up and remove a tray placed on a table.

Wait, that wasn't a table.

I hadn't even noticed them, but there, on their hands and knees, were two almost-naked guys. Steel had just lifted the silver tray off their backs. My brain was taking a minute to process what I was seeing.

What the heck was I actually looking at here?

Two cute, young guys—one slightly beefy, the other with a thick mop of black hair and the most stunningly beautiful blue eyes I had ever seen—peered up at us. Two sets of eyes that were glued to our every move.

"Hi, I'm Steel and it's my birthday," he said to them both.

The guy on the left, the bigger of the two guys, broke into a smile.

"Steel?" he repeated. "Is that your real name, or are you a porn star?"

There was a cocky arrogance in his tone, as well as a

seductive flirtiness in the way he looked up and batted his eyelashes at Steel. Ah, the careless confidence of youth.

Steel looked over at me, smiling. He was clearly loving this.

"Steel is my real name," he said, looking at the cheeky boy. "And no, I'm not in porn. I'm a lawyer."

"Oh, well, I was close," the guy replied, still smiling as widely as ever.

"How do you figure that?" Steel asked, his eyebrows pinching together. He was clearly intrigued by the brazen young man.

"Porn stars and lawyers both fuck people over for money, don't they?"

My mouth gaped open in shock. Steel erupted in a boisterous laugh. He looked over at me, his light blue eyes gleaming.

"I like this kid."

He squatted down, resting his forearms on his knees, his face inches away from his verbal sparring partner.

"And what's your name?" Steel asked, lowering his voice so that it came out deep and sexy.

"I'm Nick," he replied confidently. "And this is my best friend in the whole wide world, Mikey."

"Well it's very nice to meet you Nick...and Mikey."

Steel made a point to look over at the other guy, the one with the big blue eyes, before turning his attention back to Nick.

"Now Nick," Steel began. "I was wondering if you...and Mikey...might be able to help my friend and I out."

"Well, you are the birthday boy," Nick said, lifting his face, inching it even closer to Steel's. "You get whatever you want tonight."

His lips tugged upward seductively.

Steel slowly stood back up, keeping his gaze fixed on Nick.

"I was hoping you'd say that."

Steel tilted his head to a chair next to Mikey, as he walked over and sat on the chair beside Nick.

I had no idea where he was going with this but I made my way over and sat down in the chair, trying to keep my expression in check. What was he doing? What was he wanting me to do?

"You look tired," he repeated, again, as he looked over at me, sitting down and making himself comfortable in the chair. "And I'm a bit tired too, actually." He yawned, but it came out loud, almost fake. "What do you say we put our feet up?"

And with that, Steel toed off his shoes and peeled off his socks. A moment later, he had his bare feet in the small of Nick's back.

He leaned back in the chair, placing his hands behind his head, giving me the biggest grin of his life. I could see Nick was smiling too, looking like he was enjoying this just as much as Steel was. Whatever *this* was.

I looked down at the other young guy, Mikey.

I'd noticed his blue eyes flicking over toward me a couple of times while Steel had been talking to Nick. Every time he did, I felt a slight heat rising in my chest. Not that I was returning his gaze as intently as he was looking at me, or anything like that.

He had a tight, lean body, and I couldn't help but notice his firm, round butt displayed proudly in the air. His lower back curved downward, accentuating his ass even more. It was impossible to miss, and yeah, maybe my eyes did linger on it for a moment or two longer than they should have.

But what the hell was he thinking about us? Probably that we were a couple of middle-aged guys that should have known better. In my defense, I did know better, but it was Steel's birthday and I was trying not to be any more of a downer than I probably already was.

There was a friendliness in Mikey's eyes. A kindness. He

smiled at me, and I instantly felt some of the tension escape from my shoulders. I smiled back. He was looking at me expectantly.

Right, I was meant to put my feet on his back.

Nothing weird about that at all.

Slowly, and with great care, I took off my shoes and socks, placing them beside me. I lifted my legs and stretched them out, lightly placing the backs of my heels onto Mikey's back.

He was a lot smaller than me. I didn't want to hurt the guy or have the weight of my legs make him uncomfortable. Well, any more uncomfortable than this situation already was.

His skin was soft and supple as my feet settled into the groove in his lower back. I exhaled loudly, suddenly all too aware that I had been holding my breath, for how long I didn't even know.

"See?" Steel said, his eyes sparkling, looking as happy as a pig in mud. "This isn't so bad now, is it, Stirling?"

CHAPTER THREE

MIKEY

The hottest piece of Daddy meat in the world had a name—and what a fucking hot name it was, too.

Stirling.

It sounded so regal.

So deliciously strong.

So *I can't wait to be yelling it at the top of my lungs while he's fucking the living daylights out of me* sexy.

But perhaps I was getting a little ahead of myself.

When he had walked over to us with his friend, Stirling was standing so straight, so rigid. I kept wondering what had him wound up so tightly. I kept sneaking glances in his direction as Steel flirted shamelessly with Nick, and Nick flirted shamelessly right back.

But I couldn't get a proper read on Stirling. There was something on his mind, and I got the feeling it was more than just the awkwardness of talking to two pieces of human furniture. Although I could totally see how that would be a lot.

What I did get though, was a close-up view of him. And what a fucking view it was. If I thought he looked good from across a crowded room, up close Stirling was a walking piece of art.

The first thing I noticed when he walked over was his eyes. Those deep green, piercing eyes that I could stare into forever.

The rest of his face was just as gorgeous. Thick, short brown hair with just the faintest hint of gray at the temples, a perfect square jaw, a strong nose, and a smooth, olive complexion. All of it just radiated pure masculinity. I wanted to breathe it in for as long as I could.

But again, it was the way the man moved that sent an excited shiver bolting up my spine. His manner and movements were slow and deliberate—and unintentionally sexy as fuck. The slow-and-steady way he sat down and took off his socks and shoes sent pinpricks of heat flashing across my skin.

My body was aching for him. I wanted this man to touch me, to feel the warmth of his skin on mine. I steadied my breathing, my heart was racing so fast I thought it would fall right out of my chest and onto the floor.

I gazed up at him, and despite his steady demeanor, he looked unsure about the whole situation. Yet he also didn't object. He could have. At any point, he could have told his friend that he wasn't interested or that he didn't want to do it. But he never did.

His lips—his deliciously pink, supple lips—remained firmly sealed the whole time. So at least some part of him was interested in this.

And maybe some part of him was interested in...me?

It was moments like these that I wished I had Nick's easy confidence. He just dove right into any situation, including two handsome men coming over and asking to use us as human footstools, without the slightest hesitation.

He never doubted himself, never wondered whether somebody was as into him as he was into them, or whether he'd say something stupid and make a complete fool of himself. How did he do that?

I managed to suppress a grimace at my own lameness and instead took a deep breath and turned my attention back to Stirling.

I was nowhere near as big or muscly as he and Steel were, but I made sure to present my body in the best way possible. I tightened all of my muscles and arched my back, tilting my ass higher into the air.

It didn't go unnoticed.

I saw his eyes lingering over my body, especially my ass, and I honestly couldn't blame the man. It was an impressive ass: firm, round and inviting. I could see him swallowing hard, his Adam's apple bobbing about in his throat, as he placed his feet delicately in the curve of my lower back. He was being careful and deliberate with his movements.

So maybe it was a bit of him being slightly weirded out by the bizarreness of the situation combined with...caring?

Was he worried about me? Did he want to make sure I was okay with everything? Was he worried that a guy his size placing his feet on a guy my size could hurt me? That thought made my stomach flip with happiness.

The second I felt the flush of his skin against my skin, my cock pulsed, its firmness throbbing against my briefs. This situation—me almost naked, on my hands and knees, with this sexy man's feet on my back—was making me tantalizingly hard. It ticked so many of my boxes and just felt so right.

So, let's recap here. Strong, silent...and now caring? I was definitely letting my mind run away from me again, but it just felt so damn good. It was nice to imagine him being the kind of man I thought he was. The kind of man I wanted to be with, to submit to, to be looked after by.

I wondered what was going through Stirling's mind.

That was what I loved so much about the strong and silent type of guy. We didn't always need to talk, to ask about every single last thing. I learned to read the signs, the gentleness of a touch, or the way he looked at me and reacted to what I was saying.

It was a different way of communicating, of connecting. In some ways it was deeper.

Unlike Nick and his guy, Steel. I glanced over my left shoulder to see them chatting away nonstop. I could clearly see Steel's face and he looked like he was enjoying every single second of it, almost as much as I knew Nick was.

He had his legs stretched out on Nick's back and his hands wrapped around the back of his own neck, causing his already big bicep muscles to bulge even more. I knew Nick would be lapping up every single moment of attention the guy was giving him.

The situation with my guy, I mean Stirling, was more of a work in progress.

My guy.

That did have kind of a nice ring to it though. The *slow-the-fuck-down* button in my brain was clearly malfunctioning, damaged—possibly permanently—by my rock-hard cock pressing against my briefs.

I turned my head over my right shoulder to get a better look at my—I mean, Stirling's face. He didn't look comfortable. He was biting down hard and clenching his jaw tightly. I realized that in all of this time, we hadn't spoken. We hadn't even exchanged a casual hello with one another.

"It's okay," I said, putting on my most calm and reassuring

voice. He responded immediately, turning to look at me. "You can rest your feet down on me a little harder. You won't hurt me. Just pretend I'm a regular ol' foot stool."

I flashed him my sexiest smile, while ignoring the stupidness of the words that had just come out of my mouth.

I couldn't tell what he was thinking. His face was blank, completely unreadable. He looked down and his piercing green eyes met mine. Those eyes—fuck, I just wanted to melt into those eyes like mozzarella onto a pizza.

He shuffled in his seat to lean in a little closer. Instinctively, I drew my body closer toward him too.

"Let me fill you in on a little secret." His voice was as deep as it was husky and it filled my chest with an immediate burst of heat.

I waited with bated breath for the next words to come out of his mouth.

"I don't normally talk to my regular ol' foot stool at home."

I smiled. Strong, silent, caring...and now, funny to boot. Ding ding ding! This guy was hitting all of my buttons. Could he be any more perfect?

My mind began racing. What approach should I take with him? I didn't think that being as bold and cheeky as Nick was being with Steel would work. Stirling seemed quieter. He was more reserved. But he also hadn't hesitated too much at putting his feet on my back, so he wasn't all Mr. Sweet and Innocent either.

I turned to look at him again and I could have sworn I saw him cover his mouth and...yawn. Fuck. Was he bored? Was I boring him? Goddamnit. I had to do something, and fast, before the man fell asleep on me.

"Would you mind taking your feet off my back, please?" I cooed, in what I hoped was a seductive and sultry tone and not something that sounded like I was choking on a grape. I wasn't entirely sure. I was a little out of practice when it came to flirting, and the presence of this man so close to me was unsettling. In the best possible way.

"Of course." He lifted his feet instantly, leaving them suspended in midair, hovering just over me. I pushed myself back onto my legs and twisted around until I sat cross-legged in front of him.

Fuck staying still, I needed to take this to the next level.

A rush of blood filled my hands. It was only at that moment that I realized how much pressure had been building up around my wrists.

"Are you okay?" he asked. Concern filled his voice as I rotated my wrists around, trying to bring my hands back to life.

"Yeah, I'm good," I said, resting my hands by the sides of my body. "Here, give me your feet," I said as I patted my thighs, indicating that he should bring his feet onto my legs.

He lowered them down, slowly and with great care. Damn, I loved watching the man move. He was so sturdy and, for some reason, it had a calming effect on me.

I wasn't babbling at a million miles an hour, which was very unusual for me. I didn't feel like I needed to. His strength and his assuredness filled the gap my incessant babbling normally would, and it felt...nice.

With his feet resting in my lap, I wrapped my hands around them protectively, encasing them in my warmth. He may have looked strong and solid, but there was something else going on with him.

I had no way of knowing what it was, but it brought out my need to help, to serve.

It was my turn to ask him, "Are *you* okay?"

I looked up to study his still-unreadable, handsome face.

He looked at me and didn't say a word. In a weird way, he didn't have to. There was something about the way he looked at me, his green eyes gently meeting mine, that made me feel like I understood what was going on inside of him. Which was crazy, since I barely knew the man at all.

But at least I could tell that he wasn't bored, and I got the sense that he was slowly acclimating to the situation we found ourselves in.

I narrowed my eyes to look at him a little more closely. His eyes were framed by two dark circles underneath. He looked tired. He returned my gaze, his eyes softening as his lips curled into a friendly smile.

I felt my cheeks reddening, as if he had caught me reading his mind, as if he knew that it was filled with a million thoughts of him. I looked away, casting my gaze down to his big feet resting in my lap. They were strong, tanned feet and they rested so snugly against my body.

I looked up a little. Not all the way, but enough to see his mountainous chest heaving. The steady rhythm of his breathing calmed me even more and gave me the resolve I needed to return my gaze to his face again.

The face that had been so far away from me at the start of the evening. The face that I had been so desperate to see from across the room.

His presence made me tremble, and the steadiness of his movements seduced me, but it was his face that drew me in.

And those eyes. Those beautiful, deep green—and admittedly, a little tired-looking—eyes, were making me fall under his spell. Hard. I wanted to find out everything about him. I wanted to tell him everything about me. All of my hopes, my dreams, and all of my wildest and kinkiest desires.

As I stared into his eyes, I ran my thumb over the edge of his left foot. The firm pressure of my digit against the tight muscles on the underside of his foot surged through his body. He tilted his head back and let out a deep, guttural groan. It was the sexiest sound I had ever heard.

I wondered what he did for a living. Steel had said he was a lawyer, maybe Stirling had a high-pressure job too. Maybe that was why he looked tired. I wanted so desperately to know more about this man.

"How do you do that?" he asked, his foot trembling slightly against the firm pressure of my hand.

"Did you like that?" I replied with a knowing smile.

He nodded his head as my fingers ran across the fleshy part of his foot again. This time with a little less pressure. The man was seriously tight. I wondered what had gotten him so wound up. And I wondered what else I could do to help unwind the tight coils of stress in his body.

The look of pleasure that swept across his face flooded my body with a wave of happiness. Beaming and with a sense of inner-confidence I hadn't felt in a very long time, I ran my fingers along the top of his foot, then traced my way down along his smooth soles.

I pressed in firmly again and watched as he arched his back. I had no idea what had caused him to be this stressed and his body so tense. All I knew was that sitting there at his feet, and making him feel good, felt so right.

I knew it was crazy. I knew it made no sense. The man had entered my line of sight less than an hour ago. All of the feelings surging through my body made absolutely no logical sense. I got that, but at the same time, I didn't care.

There was something different about him, and that was setting off something very unexpected inside of me.

I continued rubbing his soft soles in silence. It was a comfortable silence. Sure, my heart was beating so hard I was sure he could hear it, but somehow I was okay with that. My need to fill the void with endless chatter about something, anything, had disappeared.

He closed his eyes. I loved seeing his massive chest rise and fall with every breath in and out. We didn't need words. There was something happening here, something between us that defied logic and sense, but it was as real as the floor I was sitting on.

Did he feel it too? What was going on inside of him? I could feel his whole body starting to loosen, to relax under my firm touch. As I looked up at him, I could see his jaw unclench and his face start to soften.

He had to be feeling this too. It couldn't just be me, could it, imagining something that I wanted so badly? Seeing only what I wanted to see?

Oh fuck, it probably was. I always did this. I always let my imagination and my desires run away with me, pulling me toward what I hoped for and wanted, while choosing not to see what was actually right in front of me. I'd done it with Brian before, was I doing it again with Stirling now?

I sighed loudly, which made him open his eyes. He looked around as if he had just woken up and wasn't entirely sure where he was. He was so freaking sexy I couldn't handle it. I smiled up at him.

"What you're doing feels so good, Mikey," he said, looking straight at me.

Hearing him say my name for the first time made my heart do cartwheels of joy.

"Good," I said, looking straight back. "I'm happy to keep going for as long—"

"Sorry to interrupt," Steel's voice cut in.

He was standing beside me. There wasn't even the slightest hint of judgement in his voice or in the look that he gave me. And trust me, I knew a thing or two about being judged.

"We need to go, Stirling. I just saw a cake being wheeled out. Sorry." He looked at me when he apologized.

"It's fine," I said, releasing Stirling's feet gently. "You are the birthday boy, after all. You're kind of needed for that whole cake thing," I said as I stood up.

"Yeah, that's usually how these things work," he said with an apologetic smile, as Stirling started to put his socks and shoes back on. Slowly, of course.

Once he was done, he stood up in front of me. He was a good four inches taller than me, which I really liked for some reason.

"Uh, thanks," he said. He opened his mouth as if to say something else, but then quickly snapped it shut.

"You're...welcome." It was all I could think of to say as Steel grabbed Stirling by his arm and the two men began to walk away from us.

Nick stood next to me as we watched them make their way across the room, rejoining their friends and turning their attention to a massive chocolate cake filled with candles, that was being brought out by two naked butlers.

"Now those are some seriously sexy Daddies."

Nick's words hung in the air between us.

"Uh huh."

It was all I could manage.

"So," Nick said as he placed his hand firmly on my shoulder, giving it a little squeeze. "That whole *I'm-over-men* thing, then?"

I didn't even have to turn my head. From the corner of my eye, I could see the shit-eating grin stretching across Nick's face.

"Yeah, totally over that." My eyes were fixed on Stirling, following his every movement. "I am one hundred percent back into men."

CHAPTER FOUR

MIKEY

You would think that a week would be a decent enough amount of time to get someone who you'd barely met, someone who had used you as a piece of human furniture no less, out of your head.

But no, you'd be wrong.

I didn't know why, but I just couldn't get Stirling out of my head.

The last time I'd seen him had been that night, after everyone had sung happy birthday to Steel. I'd seen someone hand him a piece of cake, and then that was it. He'd disappeared. He had looked tired, and I had caught him yawning, so it made sense that he had left the party early to go home.

Even though I knew it shouldn't, it did hurt a little that he hadn't come to say goodbye. Okay, maybe more than just a little. I couldn't help it. He hadn't come back over to see me or even just wave a quick goodbye. That was all I needed, to have seen him just one more time.

But then again, why would he have come over? We had only just met and it wasn't like we were being introduced to each other through friends at a party. I came into his life as a human footstool. And by the looks of things, I wasn't going to be anything more to him. So why would he have bothered to find me to say goodbye?

I had definitely felt something toward him, but in all honesty, apart from my own desperate desire, Stirling had given no indication that he felt anything toward me. Sure, maybe he'd looked at me a little longer than usual, maybe he'd looked like he was about to say something before Steel took him away...but that was all it was, a whole bunch of *maybes*.

I was doing that thing that I always did, running ahead of myself. Reality never caught up to the fantasy I created in my head, a fantasy where a guy like that, a dreamboat Daddy, would be interested in, and compatible with, a boy like me.

But this time though, it really did feel different.

A week had also made me realize that I knew nothing about my Daddy-in-shining-armor. Was I his type? Was he even single? I had no idea.

All I was left with was the memory of the most amazing eyes I had ever looked into and the feeling I had gotten when I'd sat on the floor, rubbing his feet and making his body tremble with pleasure.

It had awakened something deep and powerful within me. Something that I hadn't been able to get out of my mind for an entire week.

I let out a deep sigh as I reached the brown brick building of the Daylesford Community College. I stepped through the automatic front doors into an airy, light-filled reception area. The signs for Building C indicated that it was straight ahead, out past the courtyard.

I continued on my way as my thoughts drifted back to...who else? Stirling.

I just had to learn to accept that it was going to be another one of those one-sided things, with me being on the side that imagined things that weren't there, and I would ultimately end up hurt, disappointed, and alone.

Besides, right now I had something else to focus on. Something important, something that would have a very big impact on my future.

I was on my way to take the exam to become a childcare worker. Given that my high school grades hadn't been that great, I needed to pass an entrance exam to get into the program.

I'd been adrift since finishing school, not really knowing what I wanted to do with my life and not having any clear direction or sense of purpose. For the first year or two, it was fine. I figured that not everyone knew what they wanted to do with their lives at eighteen, so taking some time to figure things out and getting to know what I wanted made perfect sense.

But now here I was, approaching my mid-twenties and starting to freak the fuck out about it. Why was it taking me so long? Why couldn't I find what I was meant to do with the rest of my life like everyone else had? Surely life had more in store for me than being a naked butler.

But what was it? The idea came to me in the most unusual of ways, which of course meant that it involved Nick.

In addition to being a naked butler, Nick was also a clown. As in, an actual, professional clown. He was also a magician at children's parties, a go-go dancer, and he helped his grandparents out at their bakery. What can I say? The guy had a talent for odd jobs he was oddly good at.

Sometimes for his magician gigs, he would need a famulus— magician-talk for an assistant. Someone who held props and acted as a distraction while he discreetly hid rabbits and made them reappear, like magic, out of his hat. As Nick's bestest and longest friend, that so-called honor fell to me.

In all honesty, I didn't mind. In fact, I secretly kind of liked it. It was so much fun. All of his magician and clown work was at kids' parties. I just loved seeing their faces light up in amazement as he performed his tricks. It filled me with such happiness to see them smiling and delighting in the wonders of the world. They were so curious and open at that age, it made me want to be a part of it.

Being a magician or a clown wasn't that appealing to me. Nick had the bubbly personality to really make it work, and his thick body came in handy too. He really filled out those clown suits nicely.

I loved being around kids and I wanted to do something fun and exciting with them, maybe even teach them a thing or two. Becoming a childcare worker felt like a good fit. I was still basically a big kid myself anyways, so why not play to my strengths?

But first, I had an entrance exam to pass. Studying had been going well. I had been surprisingly disciplined, studying for a few hours every day, even on weekends.

Everything had been going smoothly and I was well on track...until exactly seven days earlier, when a certain breathtaking Daddy had entered my life. Ever since that night, my mind had been flooded, inundated, with thoughts of him and only him.

All sorts of thoughts, but mainly naughty ones.

What was he into? Was he vanilla or kinky? He gave off a top vibe, but I knew better than to assume someone's preferred sexual role just by looking at them. A person's physical appearance didn't necessarily dictate their preferences in bed...or in the backseat of a car, or on a kitchen table, or anywhere he wanted to take me.

What would he look like underneath me while I straddled him? What would it feel like to have him explore my body, those thick fingers tracing patterns against my skin, his tongue hungrily lapping, and what I could only imagine would be a hefty cock pushing into my body and filling me up?

See, once I had started, it was impossible to get the man out of my head.

The worst part about it, aside from not knowing whether my feelings were reciprocated in any way, was the heavy pit that had formed in my stomach and stayed there all week, once it dawned on me that I would never see him again.

Depending on how you looked at it, Daylesford was either a small city or a big town. Either way, in my twenty-four years of living there, I had never run into Stirling before. What were the odds that I would ever run into the man again? Zero. Zilch. Nada. It just wasn't going to happen.

And again, there I was thinking about him when I needed to be focusing on acing this exam. This was my future, a really important chance for me to make something of my life. As impossible as it was, I had to push him out of my brain, at least for the next hour or so, and really focus my mind on the task at hand.

I made my way over to the clearly marked Building C and strode up the stairs to the second floor. Nerves started to flutter in my stomach as I walked down the long corridor. I had this. I could do this.

I grabbed my phone to check the time. I was early. With a relieved exhale, I put my phone back into my pocket and turned the corner, colliding hard with somebody approaching from the opposite direction. I lost my balance and fell to the ground, the backpack that was slung across my shoulder falling to the ground next to me.

"Are you okay?" a deep, slightly familiar voice boomed as a strong arm reached out to help me up.

I was a little lightheaded, more in shock than actually hurt, as I reached for the hand.

My fingers slid smoothly into the hard, calloused hand, and before I knew it, a firm grip guided me back up to my feet. I steadied myself and brushed my shirt down a few times to tidy myself up a bit.

I looked at the person I had bumped into. It was a man. He was dressed in black boots, dark slacks and a checkered shirt. He had a solidly built body. I lifted my chin and found myself staring into the most gorgeous pair of piercing green eyes I had ever seen. I felt my breath catch in the middle of my chest.

Holy shit.

It was him.

The Daddy of my dreams.

Any air that was left in my lungs got vacuumed out and I struggled to breathe. I couldn't believe what I was seeing. It was him. I had literally collided with Stirling, the man I hadn't been able to stop thinking about for the past week.

I let out a giant breath, followed by a deep inhalation. I must have looked as if I were about to faint, because the next thing I knew, his arms were around me. He was propping me up, making sure I was okay.

The gentle warmth of his rough hands felt all sorts of yummy against my skin. My brain was swirling in a sweet daze of confusion, but it was switched on enough to realize that if I kept this up—this *looking like I was about to drop dead in a heap on the floor* thing—he would keep me wrapped up in his strong arms. It was beyond tempting.

"Are you okay?" he asked again, and I realized I hadn't answered him the first time.

"I'm—I'm fine," I stammered.

He looked at me intensely as he slowly took his arms away from me. Damn, why hadn't I lied and said I was about to die or have a heart attack? I could be so stupid sometimes. I missed his touch already.

"I'm sorry. I didn't see you there."

His voice was as deep and sexy as I had remembered it being, even with the concerned undertone attached.

I looked into those amazing eyes of his—those deep, piercing green eyes—and then it hit me.

He didn't recognize me.

He probably just thought I was a student at the college. He had no idea who I was. The sadness at that realization hit me harder than it should have. The way he was looking at me now, and the way he had looked at me at the party, were completely different.

"I, uh..." I tried to speak as he bent over and picked up my backpack, handing it back to me with a warm smile.

"Here you go."

His words were friendly and polite, but how the hell could he not recognize me when I had jerked off at least a dozen times to the very thought of him? I was crushed that I hadn't made enough of an impression for him to remember me one short week later.

"You don't...recognize me?" I felt like an idiot as I said it.

I could feel my cheeks heating up as he considered my question. His eyes scanned my face, darting around me, as if he were trying to place me, but was unable to.

"No, I'm sorry. You do look a little familiar though." He was speaking slowly and choosing his words carefully. "I've had a lot going on lately."

That was the most I had ever heard the man speak, and damn if his words didn't send a heavenly ripple through my

entire body. It was almost enough to offset my disappointment at
him not remembering who I was. Almost.

I forced a smile. Sometimes when life gives you lemons, you
gotta add a shitload of tequila to it and make margaritas. Or
something like that.

"Maybe you would recognize me better if I were naked," I
said.

Now it was his cheeks that were reddening. He glanced
around the corridor to make sure there was no one around.
Luckily for him, the hallway was pretty much deserted.

"Or maybe," I said, giving my lips a quick swipe with my
tongue, "you would recognize me better if you were using me as
a...footstool?"

A look of recognition instantly lit up across his face and
his eyes widened in surprise. I hoped it was a pleasant
surprise.

"Oh right, yeah, of course. You're...that guy."

"I am *that guy*, Stirling," I said teasingly, making a point to
show him that I had remembered his name.

"I'm sorry. I'm bad with names," he said, and the innocent,
puppy-dog eyes he flashed at me tugged at my heart.

It took every ounce of self control I had not to jump back
into his arms and press my body as tightly as I could against his.
With the way he was looking at me, I would have forgiven him
for anything.

"Bad with names...and faces...and bodies, it would seem," I
added cheekily, pushing my luck a bit.

He smiled and a wave of relief washed over me knowing that
he knew I was just kidding. He had looked uncomfortable and
tired at the party and I'd never gotten the chance to see his smile
close up. It was just as beautiful as the rest of him.

Okay, okay, this was going well. I was upright, fully clothed
this time, standing only a few inches away from the sexiest man I

had ever laid eyes on—and he knew who I was. Wins across the board. Now what?

A silence fell between us. He was looking at me, not saying a word. God, those eyes. Those deep, penetrating green eyes of his. I kind of wanted to break the silence, but I kind of didn't. I was curious to see where it would lead.

The quietness continued to stretch out between us. He was the silent type, after all. Which was fine with me. More than fine, actually.

I tried to kick my brain into gear, but it was about as useful as trying to open a tight jar with wet hands. I knew that at some point one of us would have to say something, and it would probably be me.

I didn't really care what I said, I only hoped that I wouldn't make a complete fool of myself. Although so far, he had used me as a footstool and seen me fall to the ground. I'd have to say something pretty big to top that.

Then it came to me.

Out of nowhere and all at once, I knew what I wanted to say. My breath hitched in my throat as the words, and the thought of me saying them to him, sank in.

I'd regretted not saying something to him the first time I saw him. I wasn't about to make the same mistake again.

But I'd never done this before. I had never needed to. This was a big deal. And sure, it kinda screwed with one element of the whole Daddy/boy dynamic, but at this point, I didn't care.

It needed to be said.

I had to say it.

That filter between brain and mouth was soundly asleep at the wheel. I took a deep breath as I raised my eyes to meet his gaze.

"Stirling."

My voice came out cracked and raspy. I cleared my throat. I

could feel myself losing courage by the second, but I didn't want to back down now.

I had to do it.

I had spent the last seven days and nights thinking about this man nonstop. If I didn't do it now, I would regret it forever. I opened my mouth and let the words fall out on their own.

"Would you like to go out on a date with me?"

CHAPTER FIVE

STIRLING

"No thanks, kid."

I had always been comfortable with silence. Words? Not so much. And this was exactly the reason why.

The words escaped me, tumbling out of my mouth before I knew what was happening.

All I knew was that one minute I was making my way back to the utility room to pick up some more supplies for the classroom my crew was renovating, and the next, I had run into someone, knocking them to the ground.

I felt bad enough about that as it was. I mean, the guy dropped to the ground like a lead balloon. It was quite the fall. I was genuinely worried he may have been seriously hurt. On top of that, I had no idea who he was.

He was right. I didn't recognize him with clothes on. He looked completely different from the guy I had met at Steel's party. He was dressed slightly preppy, in a blue button-down shirt and khaki chinos. Okay, maybe I did recognize one thing, his ass looking amazing in those tight-fitting pants.

The moment he told me who he was, though, something funny happened inside me.

A warm sensation filled my chest, and I was happier to see him again than I would have expected to be. I mean, I had only spent a few minutes with him at the party. For most of that time he had been practically naked, and I had been incredibly uncomfortable.

I had to admit it though, he was cute. And funny. And talkative. And way, way, way too young for me.

I remembered the impromptu foot rub he had given me. I'd never felt anything like it before. The pressure he'd applied to my feet had sent waves of pleasure through me and made me feel more relaxed than I had been in a very long time.

The warmth in my chest spread throughout my entire body at the memory.

For some reason, I also really liked the memory of him sitting on the floor in front of me, looking up at me with those sparkling, bright blue eyes of his. The same blue eyes that I had just crushed with my stupid words. The same blue eyes that were now staring at me, blank and hurt.

Fuck, I hated talking.

I didn't know what to say. Apart from going back in time, what could I do to make this situation better? Dammit, I felt like an idiot for blurting out what I'd said and making the poor guy look at me that way. A sadness pulled at my heart as I looked at him.

"Oh...okay," he finally stammered.

He looked down and I winced. Damn. I hadn't meant to say no. At least, not like that, so quickly and roughly.

The sharpness in my tone had more to do with me being caught off guard at seeing him again and the complete and total unexpectedness of his question. He had caught me completely by surprise.

Dating, like so many other things in my life, had been relegated to the *just-a-distant-memory* pile while my life was overrun by work and the neverending court case from hell.

I couldn't even remember the last time I had thought about going out on a date with a guy. Hearing about all the adventures that Steel, Porter, and Hudson got up to—and believe me, there was no shortage of them—was the closest I got to anything resembling romance in my life.

Yep, I was completely lame. The president, vice-president, and treasurer of Loserville. Population: me.

And Mikey probably thought I was the biggest jerk in the world. I couldn't blame him one bit.

What was I supposed to do now? He looked visibly uncomfortable and it killed me that I had made him feel that way. He kept looking down, avoiding any eye contact with me and not saying a word.

This time, I wasn't enjoying the silence between us. This time, it was killing me.

I felt a sharp, stabbing pain in my chest. I wanted nothing more than to reach out, lift his chin up so that his eyes would meet mine, say something comforting to make him feel better, and take back all of the pain I had caused. I wanted to return some of that sparkle to those big blue eyes of his.

I wanted to make this right.

But I couldn't. I didn't have the words. I knew they were in me, but they were buried too deep.

I hated that I had said no to him like that, so quickly and without any hesitation. It totally sent the wrong signal. It made it seem like I wasn't interested in him at all.

But wait, was I interested in him?

Honestly, I wasn't entirely sure. I mean, yes, he was cute in that adorable, young-looking way. He'd made me feel at ease at Steel's party, and even now, a week later, the soothing effects of his touch still lingered in my body.

I liked how carefree and fun he seemed. Fun. Another thing that had become a distant memory in my life.

But he was so much younger than me. And I was so...*almost forty*. What could someone like him, someone his age, possibly see in me?

The last thing I needed in my life was a boyfriend, emphasis on the word *boy*. But if I were to date, it certainly wouldn't be somebody more than a decade younger than me.

The thought of dating a younger guy had never even crossed my mind.

Until now.

Until Mikey, standing in front of me, looking at me with those wide, sad eyes of his.

I felt lousy and I didn't know what to do. I regretted saying no and was kicking myself for it harder and harder with each passing second.

"I have to go," he finally said. His words barely audible and his gaze still fixed firmly downward.

I chewed hard on my lip, hating the fact that I had made him feel so bad. My breath, and my words, were stuck in my throat. He started to walk away, and more than anything, I wanted to reach out and just say...something.

I wanted to see his face soften, his eyes sparkle. And I wanted to let him know that seeing him happy would have, for some strange and inexplicable reason, made me feel happy too.

Instead, I just stood there.

Frozen.

Like an idiot.

I turned around, just in time to see him disappearing through a classroom door. I took a step in his direction, then stopped myself. I wasn't about to go chasing after him. That would have just been stupid. Pathetic. Total loser behavior.

So why did I want to do it so badly? Why was it taking every ounce of self-control I had in me to not do it?

I had absolutely no idea, but I knew someone who might be able to help me figure things out. I grabbed my phone out of my back pocket as I headed to the utility room and quickly fired off a text.

Me: *Guess who I just bumped into?*
Steel: *Oprah?*
Me: *No.*
Steel: *One of the Kardashians?*

I rolled my eyes. This would go on forever if I let it.

Me: *No. Mikey.*
Steel: *Who?*
Me: *One of the naked butlers from your fortieth.*
Steel: *You're right, I never would have guessed that. Was his sexy friend with him?*
Me: *No.*
Steel: *So you're telling me this because...?*
Me: *He asked me out.*
Steel: *And let me guess, you fucked it up?*

I winced. He really did know me too damn well.

Me: *Bingo. I need advice.*
Steel: *Hmm...this might require a group effort. I'll get the guys together and we'll meet you at The Laird.*
Me: *Great. What time?*

Steel: *Let's say 9.*
Me: *So late?*
Steel: *Fine let's make it 7...grandpa.*

I smiled and let it slide.

Me: *Great. See you then.*

Hudson approached the table that Steel, Porter, and I were perched around. He was carefully balancing a tray of drinks in his hands, which he deftly placed on the table, without spilling a drop. He looked pleased as punch with himself.

"Well done," Porter commented, slapping him across his back and causing Hudson to spill his beer all over the table.

He shot Porter a dark look and grumbled something under his breath as he reached for a napkin to clean up the spill.

We were at The Laird, our favorite bar. I told the guys the whole sad story of my run-in with Mikey that day—how it had happened, how he had asked me out, and how I had completely messed things up by flat-out rejecting him.

When I was done, I was met with silence. The uncomfortable kind again.

After what felt like an eternity, Porter finally spoke up.

"How can I put this nicely?" he began.

"Try," Steel interjected, giving him an *I'm serious* look.

Steel's one-word warning worked, making Porter reconsider what he was going to say. I braced myself. I had a feeling I wasn't going to like what I was going to hear anyway.

"Hmm...Stirling, you know we all love you. We're family here, right?" Porter said, his voice low and caring.

Okay, now I was completely terrified.

"But you don't talk, man," he continued gently. "And when you don't talk, you can't expect people to figure out what you want. You do it all the time, with everyone, and based on what you just told us, it sounds like you did it again today with Mikey."

I nodded glumly.

"You're right."

"And that's not necessarily a bad thing," Steel chimed in. "Not everyone has to be loud and...obnoxious."

He looked over at Porter.

"Hey," Porter cried out. "I thought we were being nice?"

"And I thought we were talking about me?" I grumbled.

"Ooh, touché," Porter said with a smile.

"Do you like him?" Steel asked, his light blue eyes scanning my face.

"Who?" I replied.

"Chris Hemsworth. Mikey, you dipstick. Do you like Mikey?"

"I—I don't know," I said, bringing the vodka to my mouth and taking a sip. I could feel the weight of their stares on me. "What?" I said self-consciously. "Why are you guys looking at me like that?"

"Because you like him," Porter said in a sing-song voice. "Stirling likes Mikey, Stirling likes Mikey."

Could he be any more annoying right now?

"I don't," I protested, waving my hand in the air dismissively, but it sounded faker out loud than it did in my head.

"Oh my God, you really do like him," Porter said slowly, as if he were having a major revelation. "You're smiling, Stirling. Halle-fucking-lujah. For the first time in years, Stirling Bishop is actually smiling."

"Porter!" Steel and Hudson called his name out at the same time.

"I don't like him. I can't like him," I said.

"Why do you say that?" Hudson asked. His eyes were friendly, as if he were silently coaxing me to open up to them.

"I'm not into younger guys. You guys know that. I've always dated guys that were around my own age."

"Yeah, and look how that's turned out," Porter muttered under his breath.

"Porter," Hudson growled at him.

"Younger guys are immature," I continued. "They don't know what they want—"

"And do you, Stirling? Do you know what you want?" Steel interrupted.

He was challenging me, but I knew he was doing it out of love, and maybe because he was sick of me being a miserable prick, like I'd been for the last three years.

The question hit a little too close to home. It wasn't necessarily that I didn't know what I wanted; I actually did know. I just didn't know how to say it. How to put into words what I felt or what I wanted.

It was something that I'd never been able to do. Not with Richard, not with my friends, not with anyone, really. How pathetic was that? Here I was, a grown-ass man approaching forty and unable to do the simplest of things: talk.

"Look," I continued, ignoring Steel's question for now and hoping he wouldn't notice. "He's a kid in his twenties, and I'm a—"

Three voices said in unison, "Daddy."

What? No. Me? A Daddy?

"I don't know, you guys. I'm not... I couldn't... I mean... Daddy just sounds so..." I trailed off, unsure of what to say next.

"So...what?" Hudson probed. "It's okay, Stirling, you can say whatever you feel. I promise none of us will get offended."

I knew he meant it. I mulled it over in my head as I looked at the three of them. They were all Daddies and totally fine with it. Actually, more than fine with it. They were proud of being Daddies. They had no shame about it. No guilt, no fear, no anxiety. They were clear about what they wanted and what they liked, and they went for it.

Unlike me. In almost forty years, I hadn't figured it out.

Despite my three closest friends being Daddies, I had all of these strange hangups about it.

"I don't know how to describe it, guys," I said truthfully. "I guess the word *Daddy* just has such a weird, C-grade-porn connotation for me. It's like, it's not something that fits in with how I see myself."

I had no idea if I was making any sense to them.

Porter rolled his eyes.

"I've got two questions for you, Stirling," he said, slamming down his drink on the table, making it shake and earning another warning look from Hudson. "One, why the fuck are you watching C-grade porn? There are plenty of A- and B-grade options online. And two, why aren't you coming to talk to us about this stuff? We're like the Daddy counsel of Daylesford over here."

Steel and Hudson nodded in agreement.

"Alright, let me break it down for you," Porter continued, waving his arms around like a coach bringing his players in for a huddle. "Game plan time."

Steel, Hudson, and I eyed each other warily, but leaned in a little closer to hear what he had to say.

"It's a simple three-step plan. Guaranteed to work," Porter began, a politician's air of confidence ringing in his voice.

"As in money-back guarantee?" Steel asked, smiling. Porter flipped him off. "Hey, I'm a lawyer. I always read the fine print."

"Let's hear him out," Hudson, the voice of reason, countered. Then to Porter, "Go on."

"Thank you, Hudson. Well, it's pretty simple," Porter said, returning to his guaranteed game plan. "First, you need to figure out what you want. Get that sorted in your own head."

I nodded. Okay, I could do that.

"Then you need to tell him. Talk to him and let him know."

Less nodding. How the hell could I do that?

"Then, if there's agreement and consent, there's only one thing left to do."

We all leaned in closer, hanging on his every word.

"What?" I managed to croak.

A smile stretched on Porter's lips.

"Go for it!"

I gulped hard, the words ricocheting in my head.

Seeing my dazed expression, Hudson jumped in.

"Remember, Stirling, there are no rules when it comes to this. There's no such thing as a one-size-fits-all Daddy/boy dynamic. Each relationship is as unique as the two—or more—guys involved."

"That's right," Steel chipped in with a smile. "There are ninety-nine ways to be a Daddy, you just have to find the one that's right for you."

"Penny for your thoughts?" Porter asked.

I realized I had fallen silent, for how long, I didn't know.

"Just processing it all," I said, staring into the bottom of my almost empty glass. My words were met with a chorus of nods. I finished the rest of the vodka, playing with the remainder of an ice cube in my mouth. "Thanks. You've given me a lot to think about."

I meant it, and my heart swelled with love for all of them. I was so lucky to have these three amazing guys in my life.

"Anytime, Stirling. You know we're here for you, man," Porter said, standing up. "Guys, I'm sorry but I have to get going. I have an early start tomorrow. Is everything set for your fortieth?" He looked over at Hudson.

His birthday was up next, just a few short weeks away.

"Yes it is," Steel replied enthusiastically before Hudson had a chance to even open his mouth. "The largest yacht in Hideaway Bay Marina is booked for the entire night. It's going to be epic."

"I should get going too," Hudson said as he joined Porter. He walked up closer to me. "If you ever need to talk about anything, anything at all, you know we're here for you. Just reach out, okay?"

I nodded and stood up to give them both a hug.

"Thanks, I will," I said to Hudson.

Steel and I sat back down as we watched our two friends leave.

"I know you like him," Steel said, playfully nudging into me once Hudson and Porter had left.

"How?" I retorted.

"Your lips," he replied matter-of-factly.

"My lips?"

"Every time we've spoken about or even mentioned Mikey this evening, you've smiled. That's how I know."

"Oh you think so, huh?" I asked.

"Stirling," he said, unable to contain the glee in his voice. "You're doing it now."

"Doing what?" I asked.

"Smiling! We're talking about Mikey and you're smiling."

"I am not," I said defensively, folding my arms across my chest.

I pursed my lips together, suddenly becoming acutely aware of how difficult lips were to control.

"But what does it matter? It's a lost cause anyway," I said with a sigh. "I've fucked things up with him. He probably thinks I'm a complete jerk for the way I treated him today."

"Hey, it wasn't that bad," Steel said gently, trying to comfort me.

I appreciated the kind words, but they didn't change what had happened. I'd messed things up with Mikey and there was nothing I could do about it.

"And besides," I added, "it's not like I'm ever going to see the guy again. So it really doesn't matter what my lips are doing, Steel, because nothing is ever going to come out of this."

I felt Steel's hand rub my back in small circles.

"I'll tell you what," he said, leaning closer to me. "I'll bet you a hundred bucks that you will see him again."

I crumpled up my face in confusion.

"What?" I said. "You're crazy. Today was our last day working at the college, so I won't see him there again."

"Doesn't matter," Steel said with a dismissive smirk. "I am still willing to bet you that within one month, you will see Mikey again."

"Fine." I shrugged my shoulders. "But you might as well just give me the money now. There is no way we are ever running into each other again. Today was a one-off thing...and I blew it."

"So are you in?" he asked, giving me a gentle clap on the shoulder.

"Wait," I said, raising an eyebrow. "And what if, by some miracle of miracles, I do run into him again, what do you get out of the bet?"

"If you do see him in the next month and, technically, lose the bet," Steel said, as a smile began to stretch out across his face, "all you have to do is one thing."

"Oh yeah, and what would that be?" I asked, giving him my *I-know-you're-up-to-something* look.

"You have to ask him out on a date."

"Are you serious?" I asked. Steel looked at me, grinning and nodding like an idiot. "Fine, whatever," I said.

There was no way it was going to happen again. Today had been a pure coincidence.

I was never going to see Mikey again, and for some reason, that thought hurt a lot more than it should have.

CHAPTER SIX

MIKEY

It had been three weeks and two days since my heart skydived out of a plane without a parachute, hurtling toward the ground at breakneck speed, breaking into a million pieces when it crash-landed.

Not that I was being overly dramatic or anything.

Or counting the time since a certain someone had flat-out rejected me.

What was there to say that I hadn't said to myself countless times already? I was stupid to think he might be interested in me. I was an idiot for asking him out. I should have known better than to let my imagination run away with me and conjure up a future with a guy I had just met and barely knew.

I knew all of that. I had berated myself over and over until I couldn't feel any worse. I just couldn't help it. I'd really thought that this time was somehow different, that *he* was different. I'd been so certain that there had been something there between us, a spark, an interest, something worth exploring further.

But nope, I'd been wrong.

Three weeks and two days later, the rejection still stung like a motherfucker.

Nick pulled into the parking lot at Hideaway Bay Marina. The sun was close to setting and the sky was filled with brilliant splashes of orange and purple.

"It's his loss, Mikey," Nick said as he switched the engine off.

It was what he'd been saying for weeks.

I smiled meekly. "Thanks."

That was what I'd been saying for weeks.

We got out of the car and started walking to the yachts. The evening temperature was just perfect, with only the slightest breeze. The marina was absolutely gorgeous, tucked away in a picturesque little cove.

"You know they call this place Second Chance Bay?" Nick said, pulling me in close for a hug.

"Really?"

"Look around, Mikey. Most of these fancy yachts are owned by men. Older men. Older men looking for a second chance at love."

He started making kissy faces. I laughed, and it felt good. He always had a way of making me feel better.

When we got to the yacht, Hunter was already on the deck. He was sorting through some supply boxes and waved us up as he saw us approach.

"Jump aboard, guys," he said.

In addition to his classic all-American looks, Hunter was a great boss, always willing to get his hands dirty and help out whenever needed.

"You guys can get ready in the first room on the left down the stairs," he said as we stepped onto the yacht. "I've just got to finish unpacking a few of these remaining decorations and I'll be down in a minute. The guests should start arriving in about half an hour."

"Sure thing, boss," Nick said with a wave as we made our way down the stairs.

That was plenty of time. Getting undressed and putting on a skimpy, barely there apron and bow tie took no time at all.

It was covering our bodies in a shimmering glitter-infused body lotion that was the most work. Luckily, Nick and I had worked together often enough that we had become pros at that.

We'd start by doing our fronts and the parts of our own bodies that we could reach, then we'd help each other out with the backs and other hard-to-reach places. We were so comfortable with one another that there was no awkwardness to it.

Besides, there was no way in hell I was going out onto a yacht full of guys with a pasty white ass. Nope, I needed to get my glittery glow on.

Just as we were finishing up, Hunter burst in through the doors.

"We're short-staffed tonight," he said with rising panic in his voice.

"How short-staffed?" Nick asked, moving in toward him.

"Pat and Colton both just called in sick. So it's just you guys and me—and there ain't no way in hell I could pull off that outfit, so I'm on kitchen duties."

At least he still had a sense of humor.

"It's fine, boss," Nick said, waving his arm in the air. "We can help you out in the kitchen, and we'll just take out two trays at a time when we're serving. It'll be fine."

The guy was unflappable.

I, on the other hand, was flapping.

Holding two trays? On a moving yacht? Wearing the

smallest apron known to mankind with my bare ass exposed? Yeah, this had disaster written all over it.

Nick glanced over in my direction and, seeing the petrified expression on my face, walked over to reassure me.

"I'll take the drinks, Mikey," he said, placing his hand on my shoulder. "That way, you just need to carry the food."

"Okay, thank you," I said, feeling slightly relieved. At least that was something.

"And this yacht ain't going nowhere," Hunter said to both of us. "The weather report came in and it's too windy to go out, so we will be moored here at the marina for the entire party."

"Great," Nick was flashing me that wide, confident smile of his. "That will make it even easier. See, there's nothing to worry about. We got this, Mikey."

He really was the best friend a guy could have.

And he'd been there for me over the last three weeks and two days, helping me nurse my broken feelings and giving me the clarity I needed to be able to move on from Stirling and that whole...encounter.

I still shuddered at the thought of it, the sting of his rejection flooding my body with shame. How could I have been so stupid? Why did I always make such an idiot of myself?

But that was all in the past. I would never see the guy again. That much I knew for certain. So what if the memory of him burned brighter than ever in my mind? Wallowing in self-pity wasn't a crime, was it?

We finished getting ready and Nick went out with the first two trays of drinks as the guests started to arrive, leaving Hunter and me in the kitchen, madly adding pieces of cherry tomato, feta, and basil leaves onto crackers in the kitchen. Cooking wasn't exactly my forte, but you can't go too wrong with stacking crackers, right?

"You know, I actually lived at this marina for about a year

when I moved to Daylesford," he said as he put a tray into the oven.

"Ah, Second Chance Bay," I said looking over at him.

"What?" His brows pinched together in confusion.

Crap. Foot, meet mouth.

Thankfully I was saved by the kitchen doors swinging wide open. Nick bolted in, slightly out of breath and carrying an empty tray.

"Okay," he said, raising his hand in the air for dramatic effect. "The men are hungry. We need to get the food out. Pronto."

"Yep, I'm almost done here, Nick. If you want to refill drinks, I'll follow you out with food," I said, putting the finishing touches on the trays.

"Sounds like a plan." Nick placed a bunch of glasses onto the tray and began to fill them with red and white wine and bubbly. With his hands and eyes moving at a million miles a minute, he whispered to me, "I need to tell you something."

"What is it?"

He stopped what he was doing and looked me straight in the eye.

"Don't freak out, it's going to be okay."

Because, sure, no one ever freaked out when they heard their best friend say those words.

"What's going on, Nick?" I asked.

He let out a deep breath, grabbed me firmly by my shoulders, and looked me straight in the eye.

"He's here, Mikey."

"Who?"

My brain clearly wasn't keeping up.

"Stirling."

Crap, crap, crap.

"Don't worry about a thing," he said, letting go of me and turning his attention back to filling the glasses on the tray. "He's an asshole, he's a loser, and he is missing out on the best thing that's ever happened to him."

"I hope that's not one of our guests you're talking about," Hunter said with a dry smile as he walked up behind us.

"It is," Nick said, turning to face him. "One of our guests that turned down our beautiful Mikey boy when he asked him out on a date."

"Oh, I'm sorry, Mikey. That really sucks."

Hunter's face softened. He gave me a pitying look, probably without realizing that was what he was doing. Great, that was all I needed, for my boss to be pitying me.

Actually, maybe that *was* just what I needed. Maybe my boss's pity was the final straw I needed to finally start to let go and move on.

Who was this guy that I had become? This pathetic, whiny guy pining over someone who he barely even knew and who didn't like him back. Boo-fucking-hoo. That was so three weeks and two days ago. I didn't want to be *that guy* anymore.

I was a fucking catch. I was young, funny, cute-ish, and getting my life sorted. If Stirling couldn't see that, well then, Nick was right, it was his loss.

"Where is he?" I asked, squaring my shoulders and rotating my neck, warming up as if I was preparing for a boxing match. I carefully lifted up the two trays of hors d'oeuvres, making sure I had a firm grip on them both.

"Last time I saw him, he was on the upper deck," Nick replied.

"Great," I said with a wide smile. "Then the upper deck is where I'm heading."

I marched out of that kitchen with a renewed sense of my old confidence. What the hell had I been doing, moping around like an idiot? Sure, I liked the guy, but he clearly didn't like me back. So what? It wasn't the end of the world. The sun was still shining and the earth was still spinning.

I was so sick of allowing guys to treat me like crap. I wasn't going to take it anymore. I deserved to be treated better by others, but more importantly, I deserved to treat myself better, too.

I was looking hot as fuck tonight. My skin was glowing, my muscles were nice and tight, and I was having the best hair day I'd had in a long time. I was going to march myself up onto that upper deck and smile and flirt and be my all-around fabulous self.

And Stirling could just watch me and...

Eat. It. Up.

I reached the upper deck and a cold shiver ran through me as the salty breeze hit my exposed skin. I looked around and took in the breathtaking view of the boats bobbing up and down, with the sky a dull purple in the background.

The upper deck of the yacht had been tastefully decorated with strings of fairy lights, giving the place an ambient glow. Soulful seventies music played in the background and the well-dressed crowd seemed to be having a good time.

I made my way through the party, offering the guests a choice of hors d'oeuvres. I was chatty and friendly and one hundred percent convinced that the light breeze was making my hair move in all the right ways, like I was a model in a shampoo commercial.

I had this. I was confident. I was strong. I was channeling my inner-Beyonce and it was working.

And then I saw him. My breath hitched in my throat.

And then he saw me. I swallowed hard.

Our eyes met. Time...stopped.

I shook my head, literally having to snap myself out of the stronghold his gaze had placed me under. I threw my head back and laughed at whatever joke the guy I was standing next to had said, pretending it was the funniest thing I had ever heard. It was totally lame and fake, and he could probably see it from a mile away, but I didn't know what else to do.

My body buzzed to life at the sight of him, as if I had been struck by a bolt of lightning. Without realizing what was happening, I edged my way closer to him. Slowly but surely, my body was being pulled in his direction.

I felt his eyes on me the entire time, the heat of his gaze igniting me, as I slowly approached him and his three friends. I was in control here. I had the power.

Oh God, who the fuck was I kidding? I was being pulled under the torrent, unable to keep my head above water.

Keep it together, keep it together, keep it together.

I reached Stirling and his friends, and with all the energy I could muster, greeted them with an enthusiastic smile.

"Well good evening gentle—"

Right at that very moment, a massive gust of wind rose up from the water. It rushed up my legs, lifting my apron into the air and threatening to expose my cock for everyone to see.

Before I could panic, before I could even attempt to address what was happening, two strong hands quickly grabbed the material and pinned it down against my legs, holding the apron, and my modesty with it, firmly in place.

Those two strong hands belonged to...Stirling.

The warmth of his hard hands pressed against the flesh of my thighs and shot a thrill of heat up my spine.

The wind stopped. I shuffled my feet as he slowly peeled his hands off me, now that the material was in place and I was no longer at risk of exposing myself to everyone.

He stood up in that slow, methodical, utterly appealing way that he moved, and there I was, face-to-face with the Daddy of my *former* dreams.

I cleared my throat.

"Thank you," I said, in the most dignified voice I could muster, as I straightened my back and tried to regain my composure.

"You're welcome."

He flashed me a somewhat pained smile, scratching the back of his neck.

I wasn't looking at the awkwardly cute expression on his face. I wasn't noticing how his bicep flexed as he raised his arm up behind his head. I wasn't marvelling at how the lights were beautifully reflecting in those incredible green eyes of his.

Nope, I wasn't doing any of that. I was strong. I was feeling good. I had this. I hadn't spilled anything all night, my hair was on point, and my apron was down, covering what it was meant to be covering. Everything was good in my world.

I totally had this.

There was nothing that could trip me up here, random gusts of wind aside. Nope, nothing he could say or do to set me off balance. Nothing at all.

"You look good tonight," he said as he flashed a smile that could light up a thousand yachts. Or boats. Or lighthouses. Or whatever the hell it was that gets lit up at sea.

I cleared my throat and steadied myself.

"Thanks," I replied, mustering up a cool nonchalance.

The man was merely stating a fact. I did look fucking hot. I couldn't fault him for that.

I still had this. I was good.

"I'm—I'm really glad to see you again." His voice came out a low rumble.

Wait, was this big, burly man stammering...at me? Because of me? Because he was glad to see me again?

He had spoken to me and my brain knew I had to say something back, but he was kinda rendering me speechless.

Come on brain, think. Say something funny, or witty, or clever.

"That's nice," I replied. Okay, not my best, but not my worst either.

Stirling turned back to his friends. They kept glancing over at us. One of them even gave Stirling what looked like an encouraging nod.

The silence gave me a reprieve, a chance to remind myself that I was in control here. This was the guy who had rejected me, flat-out rejected me with no hesitation. He wasn't interested in me. He hadn't even recognized me with clothes on. I bit down on my lip, determined to stay strong.

He spun around, facing me straight-on, and his beautiful pink lips stretched out into a wide smile. The silence wasn't awkward like it had been when we'd run into each other at the college. It was more like the silence we'd shared the first night we met—exciting, and charged with possibilities.

Suddenly, I felt like I was an ice cream cone and he was the sun, beaming down on me on a hot summer's day. The longer I stood in front of him, the more I melted. I had to get out of there or I was going to lose it.

I smiled politely and began to back away. He reached his arm out and grabbed me by my elbow. Instantly and instinctively, I leaned into his touch.

Be strong, be strong, be strong, be strong.

"Mikey."

He remembered my name. My heart skipped a beat, overjoyed with happiness. He actually remembered my name, and damn if it didn't sound so fucking sexy coming out of his mouth.

We both took a step toward each other at the same time. He was breathing heavily and his scent, clean with an earthy edge, wrapped around me like a blanket.

"Yes?"

I swallowed hard. I looked him straight in the eye, as the sound of my heart thundering in my chest filled my ears.

Whatever he was going to say, I was determined to stay calm. I was not going to lose my shit over this man, this man who had rejected me three weeks and two days ago.

Whatever it was, whatever he was about to say, I had this. I totally had this. I was the one in control here. I heard him inhale sharply, and then the words fell from his lips.

"Would you like to go out on a date with me?"

"I still can't believe you said yes," Nick's voice boomed at me.

I had him on speakerphone as I was trying on my thirteenth pair of jeans.

"I know, it's crazy, right?" I said as I pulled the jeans up my legs. "Hey, which jeans make my ass look better? The skinny ones or the skinny-skinny ones?"

"Go with skinny-skinny."

"Cool, that's what I thought."

"Now, are you sure you want to be doing this?" I could hear his concern radiating through the phone.

"I am," I said, zipping up my jeans. They did make my ass look great. And yes, I was sure about this date.

Stirling's question had caught me by surprise and almost caused me to drop the trays I'd been holding when he asked. But there was something in the way he looked at me, something that I had felt from the first time I'd seen him. I wanted to know what that was. I had to find out.

But the man had flat-out rejected me, too, so I was going into this with my eyes wide open. He may have been the strong-and-silent kind of guy, but he had a few questions coming his way that he was going to have to answer.

I grabbed my phone and looked at the time.

"Shit, I gotta go, Nick."

"Why? You've got like fifteen minutes until he gets there."

"I know, I know. But I want to get downstairs and see him as he pulls up so I can do that whole *open the door and walk out of my building looking amazing* strut that I do. In a totally casual way."

Nick laughed. "You're too cute sometimes. Alright go, have fun, and remember, Mikey: Take. It. Slow."

We hung up and I raced down the stairs, tapping my foot against the front door of the building, waiting for him to arrive. When I saw his pickup truck pulling up, I opened the door and strode out, feeling great and looking amazing...I hoped.

I took a deep breath and opened the door of his truck, giving him a quick peck on the cheek. His jaw was lightly stubbled, leaving a pleasant tingling sensation on my lips.

"So, where are we going?" I asked with a slight bounce as he pulled out.

CHAPTER SEVEN

STIRLING

"You're going to kill me, aren't you?"

I grinned as I looked over at Mikey who was sitting in the passenger seat. He looked more adorable than terrified. I noticed him the second I pulled up outside his apartment building. He bounced out with such excitement that it left me even more speechless than normal.

"I'm not going to kill you," I said reassuringly, turning my attention to the open road in front of us.

"Well, I don't know you at all, Stirling. You could be a serial killer," he said.

"Alright, what would you like to know? You can ask me anything," I said.

He didn't even wait a full second. "Your full name?"

"Stirling Bishop."

"No middle name?" he asked, eyeing me up and down with mock-suspicion. He was taking this grilling seriously.

"No, no middle name."

"Good," he replied, settling back into his seat a little.

"Why is that good?" I asked.

"Because lots of serial killers have middle names."

"Like who?" I snickered.

"Like John Wayne Gacy or...Jack the Ripper."

"Jack the Ripper. What, you think his middle name is *The?*" I chuckled some more, and from the corner of my eye I could see Mikey smiling too. A smile that spread a warm feeling across my chest and down into my belly.

This was, hands down, the best bet I had ever lost.

I had known Steel was up to something when he bet me that I'd see Mikey again. After all, he was the one who had booked the same naked butler company for Hudson's birthday party on the yacht. I should have caught on earlier.

As it turned out, he had even specifically requested that Nick and Mikey work that night. But what are best friends for if not to deliberately set you up to lose a bet so that you'd have to ask a sexy-as-hell naked butler out?

The whole *asking-somebody-out-on-a-date* thing was a whole lot more nerve-racking than I remembered it being. Probably because the last time I had asked somebody out was over a decade ago.

But when our eyes met on the upper deck of the yacht that night, a spark of lust ignited within me. I half expected the guy to either turn around and never look at me again, or walk straight up and punch me in the face. I wouldn't have blamed him either way. He had every right in the world to be completely pissed at me.

Instead, and luckily for me, a smile had bloomed on his face. He'd looked radiant, and my eyes were glued to him as he casually inched closer and closer to where I was standing.

When a gust of wind threatened to lift his tiny apron up—

Marilyn Monroe flying-skirt style—and his eyes widened in horror, I didn't even think. Something inside of me just clicked into place and I moved, quickly grabbing the material and palming it down, pressing it against the soft, smooth skin of his thighs.

Once the wind had died down, I let go of him and instantly missed the warmth of his body against my hands. As I stood up straight, a feeling of want and desire brewed in my belly. A feeling that I hadn't felt in years. A feeling that was threatening to overtake me, unless I did something about it.

Which I had every intention of doing.

My jaw clenched tightly as I waited for him to respond to my question, and my chest was gripped by an all-too-familiar tightness. But there was something else going on as well, another emotion that I was feeling, slowly bubbling its way up to the surface. Hope.

When his eyes softened and he finally said yes, my heart melted a little. Okay, a lot. My heart swelled with so much happiness I thought it would pop right out of my chest.

As I took the turnoff, it struck me just how much I had been looking forward to this very moment, to seeing Mikey again.

He jumped into the passenger seat and gave me a quick peck on the cheek. It was so quick and casual, and probably meant nothing to him, but it surprised me in the best possible way. The quick, soft touch of his lips on my cheek made me smile as we drove to one of my favorite places just outside of Daylesford.

It was a beautiful Saturday morning. The sun was shining, there was just the slightest hint of a breeze, and there wasn't a single cloud in the perfect blue sky. That boded well for visibility. I was excited, hoping that we got the chance to see some real beauties today.

I'd wanted to do something more interesting than the usual dinner-and-a-movie thing for our first date. I thought it would be a good idea to show Mikey a little bit of who I was and what I liked. And this was one of my all-time favorite things to do.

I had been mulling over the advice the guys had given me. They were right. I knew I had to talk and open up more. I couldn't expect people to figure out what I wanted without telling them, and I didn't want to continue being disappointed by not getting what I needed.

And they were also right about me needing to figure out what it was I wanted. I mean, I needed to figure that part out first. I liked what Hudson and Steel had said, that there weren't any one-size-fits-all Daddy/boy relationships. It was almost a relief, knowing that I didn't have to try to mold myself into something I wasn't.

The more I thought about it, the clearer sense I got of what I needed. I could feel it there, just under my skin. It was close enough for me to feel and right on the tip of my tongue for me to say. And maybe Mikey could be the guy that I could say it to.

I was hoping real hard that he was.

But I also knew myself well enough to realize that I wouldn't become the world's greatest conversationalist overnight. That just wasn't realistic and I didn't want to pretend to be someone I wasn't. That wouldn't be fair to either one of us. But I could still get to know him, and let him get to know me, in other ways.

I wanted Mikey to get to know the true me, not some made-up version of myself. I was too old to play games like that.

I wanted to share something with him that was special to me, and that showed him a little of who I was.

Mikey was done grilling me, and instead, he was talking away, keeping the conversation going all by himself. Mikey liked talking and I liked listening to him. He was funny and smart and interesting. And the more he spoke, the more my misgivings about dating a young guy disappeared.

As we made our way closer to our destination, I learned that he was born and raised in Daylesford. He was twenty-four years old, and was applying to study childcare and that he had been taking the entrance exam the day we bumped into each other at the community college.

I also discovered that we both had small families, but unlike me, he was close with his. He had a mom and an older brother. They both lived in Daylesford and he saw them at least once a week for dinner. There was something about knowing that he had people in his life who loved and looked after him that filled me with a sense of comfort.

Our eyes met briefly and we both smiled. I turned my head, forcing myself to keep my eyes on the road, but it was hard. The more he spoke, the more those wide blue eyes pulled me in.

I'd been looking forward to this date from the moment Mikey had agreed to it. Sure, the guys gave me shit for the rest of Hudson's party, saying I couldn't wipe the smile off my face. But it was worth it. I finally had a chance at having some fun and seeing where things might lead. I was ready for it. More than ready, actually.

Screw playing it safe, I wanted to see where going for it would take me.

"Well, can you at least give me a clue?" Mikey asked as the road became narrower, steeper. We were encased by a dense green forest on each side. I opened the windows so we could take it in. The air was thick with resin, moss, and earth.

He opened his mouth and his lips parted ever so slightly. He was taking in the fresh air. His nose scrunched up, eyes darting around trying to figure out where I was taking him.

"I have pepper spray, just so you know."

He feigned seriousness but his eyes shone with a cheeky playfulness as he returned to his *are-you-a-serial-killer* theme from earlier. His slightly inappropriate sense of humor was one of the things I was really starting to like about him.

"Well, that's good to know," I said with a grin. "But let me repeat myself, I am not going to kill you, Mikey."

He pushed back into his seat, folding his arms across his chest. His lips pushed out into the most tempting pout ever.

"Good," he said, injecting a cocky attitude into his voice. "I'm way too cute to die this young."

He licked his lips.

Did he realize how sexy he was? Was he doing it on purpose? Could he see the effect it was having on me?

I had the sudden urge to pull over onto the side of the road and taste his smiley, pouty lips for myself. But I had to show some restraint. I may have been a little rusty on the whole dating thing, but I remembered enough to know that the kiss usually came at the end of the date, not at the beginning.

Instead, I reached my hand over and placed it on his leg, just above his knee. I could feel his warm flesh underneath the denim.

"Is this okay?" I asked.

I wasn't trying to make a move on the guy. Something inside of me just felt like it was the right thing to do, that it might reassure him in some way.

"Yeah. It's...nice," came his reply. "Really nice."

His tone was even and calm, his eyes glued to the road ahead of us.

I was trying to stay focused on driving but I wanted to double-check and make sure he wasn't just saying that. I glanced over at him. He was smiling, his shoulders had eased away from his ears, and a look of contentment was spread out across his face.

This whole going-for-it thing was turning out to be pretty fucking awesome. Why hadn't I done this earlier?

We pulled into the parking lot of the Daylesford Wildlife

and Bird Sanctuary. I looked over and saw the confused expression on Mikey's face.

"We're going...birdwatching?"

"Sure are," I replied happily as I pulled into an empty spot. "There's a bit of a hike as well. Nothing too long though. We'll make our way up to the lookout."

I didn't want to tell him that it was the best view of the mountain ranges that framed Daylesford. That would be a pleasant surprise I wanted him to discover for himself when we got there.

"There's a great restaurant at the lookout, but I think it may be closed for renovations at the moment," I added.

I could see Mikey thinking it over. He was quiet. I could tell that wasn't a good sign.

A heaviness formed in the pit of my stomach. What if this wasn't such a great idea after all? What if he hated this and thought it was lame? That I was lame? My body suddenly flooded with all the fears and insecurities I thought I'd left behind in my awkward, angsty teenage years.

I knew birdwatching wasn't exactly everyone's idea of a great time, but it was one of my all-time favorite things to do. For me, there was nothing better than being outside, in the beauty of nature, enjoying the peace and the stillness, and on a lucky day, getting rewarded by seeing some of the spectacular birds that called this beautiful part of the world home.

"Birdwatching is a quiet thing, right?" he asked, unbuckling his seatbelt and turning to face me. His tone was measured.

"Yes, it is," I said with a nervous chuckle. "Being quiet definitely helps."

His mouth opened and closed a couple of times before he finally spoke.

"Isn't the point of a first date that we get to know each other? How can we get to know each other if we aren't allowed to talk?"

I could see the nervousness in his big blue eyes, but a part of me was also happy. I was glad that he trusted me enough to tell me how he was feeling. Even if he was worried that it might not be something I wanted to hear.

"There are other ways of getting to know a person, Mikey. But we can talk. Just more quietly, that's all," I replied with a steady breath and a warm smile.

I looked over at him and we stared into each other's eyes for a few moments without saying a thing.

The air hummed between us. There was definitely a spark there. I hoped he was feeling it too.

"Do you trust me?" I asked, breaking the silence.

He thought about it for a moment before nodding his head vigorously. I appreciated that he wasn't just agreeing to it for the sake of agreeing with me. His willingness to push through whatever hesitation he was feeling sent a warm feeling into my chest. It was that same feeling again...hope.

"Alright," I said as a smile spread across my face. "Let's do this. It'll be fun, Mikey."

CHAPTER EIGHT

MIKEY

I had a weird feeling in my gut as I got out of the truck. Birdwatching, fun? I wasn't exactly a huge fan of birds and all that nature-type stuff, but the smile on Stirling's face was something else. He was practically beaming. He clearly loved it, and I was determined to at least give it a try.

Stirling hadn't said a lot so far. I had done most of the talking during the drive there. But slowly, instead of using words, he was showing me the type of man he was—kind and considerate, gentle yet strong. I'd felt it in the way he'd placed his hand on my leg. He hadn't been making a move, he'd just been reassuring me.

Even this birdwatching thing was his way of sharing a part of who he was, and showing me that he was someone I could actually trust.

The word echoed around in my head like a silver ball in one of those old-school pinball machines.

Trust.

I'd had it broken before, broken so badly, yet I desperately wanted to feel it again. That warm wave of surrender and vulnerability when I really allowed myself to trust somebody else and give myself fully to them—mind, body, and soul.

The voice in my head warning me to slow down was being totally drowned out by another voice that was telling me this felt so fucking right.

Part of me felt that Stirling was feeling this too. He had it in him, I could tell. That protective instinct, that deep desire to care for someone. Maybe I was running ahead of myself in typical Mikey fashion, or maybe, just maybe, he truly was someone that I could open up to and allow inside.

One way or another, I was determined to find out. And if birdwatching was the way to do it, then bring on the birds!

Stirling took out a big brown backpack from the back of his truck and flung it over his wide shoulders. We walked over to the entrance and started on our way. I was a city boy through and through, so I was taking it all in as we walked the trail, side by side. It was nice, lush and green and surprisingly noisy too, with loud bird sounds filling the air around us.

We walked without saying anything, but I could see him looking over in my direction every once in a while, silently checking in to see if I was okay. I was...I think. A lot was going through my mind, but I was trying to slow down and not let myself get caught up in the wind gusts of my thoughts.

"You okay?" he asked gently.

I didn't say anything. I looked over at him and smiled as I slipped my hand into his. His heavy palm felt so good wrapped around my fingers.

We continued walking in silence and slowly, I started to get used to it. The clean fresh air filling my lungs, the gravelly footpath underfoot. My mind was quieting down too. Maybe it was all the nature or maybe it was Stirling's calming presence. Either way, I liked it. It was all...kinda nice.

"Holy shit," I said a few minutes later. The trail had come to an end and the dense forest opened up to one truly breathtaking peak. "This is so beautiful."

The view of the mountains stretching out until they disappeared into the horizon was spectacular. I'd never seen anything like it in my life.

Stirling slung the backpack off his shoulders and knelt down beside it on the ground, slowly unfolding a blanket for us to sit on.

"Water?" he asked, reaching into the backpack and pulling out a bottle.

"Thanks," I said, taking the bottle from him as I sat down next to him on the blanket, still in awe of the incredible view. He put his arm into the backpack, his face contorting super cutely as he shuffled around for a bit until he pulled out a black...something. "What are those?"

"They're binoculars," he said with a smile, which quickly faded as he followed up with, "You have seen these before, right?"

"Nope," I replied as I studied them carefully. He reached out, handing them to me. "They look kinda weird. Oh geez, and they're heavy too."

Our fingers gently grazed each other and my heart fluttered at the touch.

I looked at the heavy, weird binocular things in my hand, then lifted them up to my eyes and looked to the sky. It was pitch black.

"How do these work? Am I meant to be seeing anything?"

I was met with silence, then the deepest, sexiest rumble of a laugh I'd ever heard in my life.

"You're holding them the wrong way, Mikey. Want me to show you how they work?"

He didn't need to ask me twice. I scooted across the blanket to his side, the warmth of his body radiating against my skin.

He showed me how to focus the lens and covered a few other basics, such as which end was the looking-through end, but I kinda wasn't listening. I was too busy watching him, studying his face and all the subtle little movements he made when he talked, like the way he'd moisten his lips with his tongue when he was talking about something he was excited about. Or how his eyebrows would pinch together slightly as he concentrated.

"Want to give it a try and see if we can spot some birds?" he asked.

"Uh, sure," I said, taking the binoculars and holding them the right way around.

At least I'd remembered that much from what he'd said. He wrapped one of his big arms around me, pressing my body snugly into his. Quietly, he began whispering and pointing to where I should be looking.

I lost track of time but what I noticed most was how his body would twitch with excitement whenever a bird came into view. It was a subtle movement, but I could feel it. Our bodies were so close together, I could feel every movement he made and it felt wonderful.

There was a gentle jerk when he pointed out a bright red northern cardinal. He tightened his grip on me when we saw a bluebird. And he almost jumped at the sight of a black-and-gold varied thrush.

I was fast becoming a massive fan of birdwatching.

After a while, I put the binoculars away and we lay down on the blanket, staring up at the cloudless blue sky. When I turned to look at him, his face was relaxed and his mouth was open slightly. For a moment, I thought of saying nothing and just letting it go. But I knew that I couldn't. I had to find out.

"What is it?" he asked in that low rumble of his as he turned his head, his gaze meeting mine.

My stomach twisted with a mixture of nervousness and lust. It wasn't too late to back out now, I could just come up with something lame and totally let this go. But no, I bit down hard. I knew I had to do it.

"Can I ask you something?"

"Sure, anything," he said, nodding.

I hesitated and took a breath.

"Why did you say no when I asked you out?" A darkness filled his eyes. "Look, I'm not trying to make a big deal out of it or anything," I added quickly, hoping that I hadn't fucked up the moment completely. "I just, I just...need to know. Was it something I did? Did I do or say something wrong? Am I not...?"

"Stop."

The deepness of his voice stopped my mouth in mid-sentence. That was not an easy feat.

We stared at each other. My heart was in my throat. Things had been going so well, why did I have to ruin everything with my big fat stupid mouth?

Stirling reached out and gently pulled my hand into his.

"You did nothing wrong, okay, Mikey?"

I opened my mouth to say something but he raised a finger and my mouth snapped shut. I had asked the man a question, I needed to give him a proper chance to respond.

He let go of my hand and moved himself up until he was leaning on his elbow, his green eyes focused on me like a laser.

"I was an idiot and I made a mistake for saying no to you like that. I regretted it the moment I said it."

His words filled me with relief and some of the tension in my shoulders eased slightly.

"You caught me by surprise. I ran into you and you fell. I thought I'd hurt you and..."

He looked away. I could tell what he was thinking and I knew he didn't want to say it. Good thing I had zero filter.

"And then you didn't remember who I was?" I said with a devilish grin.

Hey, it had happened. There was no point in denying it. We couldn't change it, so we might as well laugh about it. Stirling looked back at me but he wasn't laughing. His expression was deadly serious.

"I'm sorry," he said, his voice husky and raw. "I'm sorry I didn't recognize you straight away, Mikey, and I'm sorry I said no. I didn't mean to hurt you. I'm just not, you know, all that great with words."

He looked at me, like he *really* looked at me, and I could see the sadness pouring out of him.

"Hey," I said, tracing my fingers delicately along his jaw. "You were pretty good with those words."

Just the faintest hint of a smile permeated the corner of his mouth.

"Thank you for telling me that. I needed to hear it and I needed to ask. If this, us, whatever...if something is going to happen here, I need to know that I can trust you," I said.

He nodded, before saying the words that I thought would turn me into a human pile of mush.

"You can trust me, Mikey. I won't hurt you again."

And then he leaned in, slowly, steadily. First I could smell him, his scent was earthy, with the faintest hint of lemony soap. And then I tasted him as his full lips gently pressed into mine. A moan escaped me and I rocked my head back, inviting him in further.

He opened my lips with his tongue as he ran his thick fingers along the top of my chest. His tongue flicked into my mouth, gently at first. As his hand reached my neck, his tongue probed in deeper. The touch of his fingers against my skin, and his tongue inside me, lit a fire that tore through my body.

I dragged my fingers through his thick brown hair and pulled him in closer. Our breathing, our tongues, were intertwined with one another. I ran my hands over his broad shoulders and down his strong, muscular back.

Eventually he gently pulled away, and lay down beside me. His eyes were softer around the edges and his lips were swollen. I had just had my first kiss with Stirling Bishop, and my heart was dancing like crazy in my chest.

I was proud of myself. I'd done it. I asked him a question that had the potential to blow up in my face. But if I was going to trust him, *really* trust him, I wanted to be sure that he was an honest man. His answer showed me that he was.

I leaned into him and closed my eyes. He wrapped me up in both arms, my head bobbing up and down on his chest with his breathing, the rhythm steady and constant. The sounds of the rustling trees got louder as the bird noises faded into the background. My eyelids drooped, getting heavier and heavier.

When I next opened my eyes, I was tucked into Stirling's shoulder with my head on his chest. I looked up at his face. His eyes were closed. We must have fallen asleep. I began to slowly pull myself away from him, the movement waking Stirling up too.

"Did we just fall asleep?" he asked groggily, with one eye still closed.

"Looks like we did," I replied with a nod.

I lay back onto his shoulder with the biggest smile on my face. I couldn't believe I had been worried about this when we first pulled up to the bird sanctuary. It had been the best, chillest first date ever. Birdwatching was fast becoming my favorite thing ever.

I buried myself further into his shoulder. I could get used to this.

"Can we do this again?" his voice rumbled against my cheek, which was resting on his chest.

"What, birdwatching?" I asked.

His chest rose. I couldn't see it, but I could feel his smile. That made *me* smile.

"Well, that would be nice, but I meant a date. Can I see you again?"

Oh, I could definitely get used to this.

CHAPTER NINE

MIKEY

Stirling had three days in the courtroom with Steel for a case, and had to somehow fit in a full workload around that, so it was a week—*seven whole freaking days*—until I could see him again. But it was worth the wait.

I was five minutes late because I wanted to make sure he was there so I could do that whole *walking down the street looking amazing* strut that I did...in a totally casual way, of course.

As predicted, Stirling was waiting outside of Betty's Diner, looking casually striking as always, in a pair of dark pants and a light blue polo. The blue looked good against his tanned skin. He smiled when he saw me approach and I felt an instant heat rush through my body.

Oh, it had definitely been worth the wait.

When I reached him, his green eyes sparkled as he pulled me into a warm embrace.

"Great choice, I love this place," he said. "I'm not big on fancy food, and they do the best burgers in town here."

I beamed, proud that my choice of restaurant made him so happy.

We stepped into the diner and made our way to an empty booth in the corner. The place was unusually empty, but that was more than fine with me. I had a few non-PG-rated things I wanted to talk about, so the fewer people around us, the better.

Stirling led the way. I loved walking behind him, watching the man move. His broad shoulders, steady; his back, a mountain of strength; his ass, holy shit. It was all I could do to keep my hands by my sides and not reach out and hungrily grab those solidly packed, full, fleshy cheeks.

Everything about him dripped of masculinity and strength. It was intoxicating.

The server appeared before we'd even sat down, menus under one arm. We both ordered burgers and fries. I added a strawberry milkshake for good measure. I'd had friends tell me how your metabolism screeches to a grinding halt as you get older, so I was determined to make the most of my twenty-four-year-old metabolism while I could.

Once the server walked away, I tapped my fingers against my thigh in excitement.

As much as I had loved our date at the bird sanctuary, I had been waiting all week for this. Getting to this part, the talking part. I was good at this. Talking was my forte, my speciality. I had a plateful of carbs on the way and the undivided attention of the world's sexiest Daddy. This was going to be good.

I had a long list of questions that I wanted to get through. I wanted to know everything I could about this man. Like where he grew up, what his favorite food was, whether he was a boxers or briefs guy, his hopes and dreams for the future, whether he was a neat freak or messy, what his favorite Beyonce song was, whether he was a get-to-second-base-on-a-second-date kinda guy, what he'd like to do to me...

Okay, *slow down, slow down, slow down.*

Good, my brain was still online and functioning. Instead of asking all of that, I took it easy.

By the time the server arrived with my milkshake, I'd learned that he had grown up in Daylesford just like me. He'd gone to Daylesford University and majored in business, where he'd met his three closest friends, Steel, Hudson, and Porter. He owned his own construction company, and a small house on the outskirts of town that he was hoping to renovate someday. His dad was still alive, but they weren't close.

When I asked him about past boyfriends, he said he'd only had one major, long-term relationship. It had been with a guy called Richard, and had ended because Richard cheated on him. He said that last part quietly, dipping his head slightly. I could see his jaw pulsating as he clenched it down tight, before he looked up at me and forced a smile. But it wasn't a real smile, there was too much pain behind it.

I felt terrible for him. Brian had been, and still was, an asshole in so many ways, but at least I could say he hadn't cheated on me. Cheating was one of the scummiest, grossest things you could to do a person, and my heart felt Stirling's pain. How could anyone ever cheat on this amazing man?

"What about you?" he asked, clearing his throat and sitting up a little straighter. "What's your deal?"

I raised an eyebrow.

"What's my deal about what?"

"Men." He said it so simply.

Then he dragged his eyes up and down me, releasing a shiver of anticipation up my spine. There was nothing simple about that. Heat pooled in my belly as I shuffled uncomfortably in my seat.

Damnit, I was meant to be good at this whole talking thing, and here I was, rendered completely speechless by this man. There was a spark in his eyes, but there was a softness there too. It was like he sensed I needed some time and he was giving it to me.

"I've recently come out of a bad relationship too, about three months ago. Well, actually, it was a so-so relationship with the breakup from hell."

I figured there was no point in sugarcoating it.

"I'm sorry to hear that, Mikey." His voice was genuine. "So this guy, was he...older?"

I smiled. He didn't normally say a lot, but when he did, he was direct. I liked that.

"Yes, he was actually. I've had three semi-serious relationships, and they've all been with men who are older."

"So, you like older guys?"

The man was on a roll. His face was unreadable as usual, but there was a curiosity in his eyes. He was sitting up straight and leaning forward, ever so slightly, invested in everything I was saying.

"Yeah, I do. But, well...some of them..."

I stopped, not sure how much I wanted to reveal here.

"Go on," he encouraged gently.

"I like older men. I do. It's just that some of them are kind of...immature, you know? They don't actually know what they want."

Stirling's eyes widened in surprise and for a moment, a flash of panic surged through me. Had I said something wrong? Was I out of line? But just as quickly, his face reset as if nothing had happened.

"What about you?" I asked. "Are you into boys?"

He may not have said *Daddy* yet, but I wasn't going to shy away from saying *boy*.

For a moment he looked like he was about to choke, but instead, he brought his knuckle to his mouth, deep in thought.

"I've never dated a younger guy before. Richard was three months younger than me, but I guess that doesn't really count, does it?"

I shook my head and smiled. Three months didn't count, especially when there was at least a good decade and a half between us. The age difference didn't bother me in the slightest. If anything, it turned me on. But since Stirling had never dated a younger guy before, I worried that it might bother him.

"So this is your first time with a younger guy?" I asked.

His eyes grew stormy and his brows pressed together tightly as he looked at me with an intensity I had never seen before.

"That's right." His voice was low and deep.

I swallowed hard.

"So...I guess that makes you..." I let the words linger in the air between us, daring him to respond.

"Makes me a what?" he asked.

I smiled a wicked smile. He'd taken the bait.

"A first time Daddy!" I said it with such glee that he burst out into a deep, rumbling laugh.

His chest and shoulders rocked and his face shone brightly. I loved the sight of it. The big, strong man who was always so controlled, so steady and put together, laughing and looking so happy and free.

"As long as I don't get arrested for dating you, you can call me whatever you like," he said, chuckling.

I stopped laughing and my brain froze. *He wanted to date me?* Holy shit. Please, please, please don't let that just be a slip of the tongue.

"Here you go, two burgers and fries." The server placed the food in front of us. "Can I get you boys anything else?"

"We're good, thank you," Stirling—who was *so* not a boy—

answered, and she turned to walk away. "Wow, that's the most I've spoken in a long time. I think my mouth's sore."

There was a bad joke in there, but I decided it wasn't the right time. Ah, so this was what it felt like when my brain decided to cooperate and act normal.

We ate in silence for a while. The burger was criminally good and over chewy mouthfuls of greasy goodness, I considered words.

Okay, so, a first-time Daddy. I could deal with that. But what sort of Daddy did he want to be? What was he looking for in a relationship, in his boy?

So far, he knew that I was attracted to older men, and I knew that he had never dated a younger guy before. But age was only one part of it. There was a whole lot more to the Daddy/boy thing.

As soon as the server was out of earshot, I went back into it. I wanted to know, no, I *needed* to know what sort of relationship this man wanted.

"So," I asked, trying to sound casual, "what do you know about Daddy/boy relationships?"

Stirling put down his burger and carefully wiped the corners of his mouth. I couldn't tell if he was really making sure he had nothing on his lips or if he was buying some time. It was probably a bit of both.

"Well, my three closest friends are Daddies," he began. "So, there's that."

He smiled again. It was still a little forced but it wasn't pain that was behind this smile. It was more like he was uncomfortable.

I knew he was the strong, silent type, but we still needed to talk about a few things. I had to find a way to stop myself from running ahead of myself and that meant talking. Also, I didn't want to have to keep guessing what the Daddy I was with wanted, I needed to hear it from the man himself.

Oh, hello maturity. Nice to finally meet you.

"I'm open to it. I like you and I'm eager to see where this goes. Honesty is important to me. No lies. No deception." He sat back a little further in the booth and looked at me. There was so much going on behind his eyes. "What about you?"

"Well, as you know, I'm a boy and I do like older men." He nodded as he was chewing. "And look, there's no one way to approach this. I have friends who are boys and their relationships with their Daddies are all very different."

"Different how?" Stirling asked.

"Well, one friend, he's a boy twenty-four seven. His Daddy makes all of his decisions for him, what to wear, what to eat, where they go out."

"Oh," Stirling said, diving back into his burger.

"Another friend," I continued, "is almost the exact opposite. He's only a boy in the bedroom. Outside of the bedroom, he's completely independent. He makes all his own decisions, and his Daddy wouldn't even dream of ordering a meal for him or suggesting what he should wear."

"Oh... And what about...what about you?"

Stirling devoured the last bite of his burger and licked his fingertips clean, making my cock twitch at the sight.

"I'm—I'm..."

God, he really had a way of making it hard for me to talk. Memories of Brian came rushing back. I'd told him what I wanted. I'd told him more than I'd ever told anyone else and then he'd thrown it all back in my face. I couldn't do that again. I trusted Stirling, I did. But I wasn't ready to tell him everything...at least, not just yet. Relationship stuff was fine, but the bedroom stuff...no. I wasn't ready for that.

"I like a balance," I began. I picked up a fry, nibbling on the end of it. "I like making my own decisions, but I also like being able to lean on someone for guidance and support, you know?"

Stirling nodded his head.

"I do like being taken care of and looked after a bit too," I added cautiously. I could feel my body start to shake. I felt vulnerable, exposed.

Before I knew it, I was being wrapped up in two solid, strong arms. Stirling had come across and sat down on my side of the booth. I leaned into his warm body, my head resting on his shoulder. Straight away, I felt calmer, my body melting into his. My vulnerability replaced with safety. My shakiness replaced with softness in my heart...and a hardness in my pants.

Stirling pulled back and gently lifted my chin with the middle of his index finger. I met his gaze. The storminess in his eyes was gone, replaced by a gentle warmth.

"Thank you for telling me, Mikey. And thank you for trusting me."

I leaned up and planted a kiss on his lips. Those soft, full lips that had been calling me, begging me to kiss them all night.

At first, he was taken aback, but within seconds, his warm tongue was exploring my bottom lip, gently sliding along it. He was taking his sweet time tasting me. I felt two strong hands on the sides of my face, and he pulled me in even closer.

I may have made the first move, but he was in control now. His tongue continued exploring my lips with a softness I'd never experienced before. Stirling was a man who took what he wanted, and I was happy to be taken any way he liked.

As my mouth opened to release a groan, his tongue charged in, hot and demanding. It swirled against mine, and everything in the world faded to black. There was no diner. No trust issues or cruel ex-boyfriends. No fear or rejection or insecurities. Nothing else existed.

It was just me and him.

Warm hands.

Hungry lips.

This kiss.

He pulled away from me.

We sat there in that booth, in the almost-empty diner, just looking at each other as it dawned on me that I had been right about him. He was a different kind of Daddy. The good kind.

Eventually, he made his way back to his side of the table. The conversation remained light for the rest of the meal, which we managed to devour in no time at all.

"You up for some dessert?" the most delectable, mouth-watering Daddy asked me as the server was clearing our table.

"Sure," I managed, and nodded enthusiastically to his suggestion of sharing a banana split. "With extra cream, please."

That wasn't me talking, that was my twenty-four-year-old metabolism.

CHAPTER TEN

STIRLING

The waitress arrived with our dessert, putting a pause on the conversation. We each grabbed a spoon and Mikey dug in with a joyful enthusiasm that made me smile on the inside...and on the outside too.

"What?" he asked, his spoon frozen halfway to his mouth. "Why are you smiling at me like that?"

"No reason, I just like looking at you."

That seemed to have done the trick, because he proceeded to devour one mouthful after the other. I did like looking at him. The dark gray of his shirt made his face and arms look even more porcelain white, almost angelic. Although I could tell there was something more going on underneath that innocent-looking face.

And I liked listening to him talk. I had to say that by my standards, I had done a lot of talking so far. It may not have seemed like a lot to anyone else, but for me, it was. Mikey made me feel comfortable enough to just open up.

I could tell he'd been dying to get to know me better. Mikey was a lot of things, but subtle wasn't one of them. He practically lunged into what I suspected were pre-planned questions as soon as we'd placed our orders.

Surprisingly, it didn't bother me. This was who he was. He accepted me, my quietness, and my fondness for birdwatching, as I was getting to know and accept things about him. Like his total lack of subtlety. It felt good.

It felt right...although his comment about older guys sometimes being immature almost knocked me out of my seat. That's what I'd always assumed—incorrectly, I could see now—about younger guys. Steel was right, age was just a number. Mikey was expressive and knew what he wanted and he wasn't afraid to say it.

Although I did pick up on something...just the slightest bit of hesitation when I asked him about what kind of Daddy/boy relationship dynamic he was interested in. He answered, but after a few moments his expression changed. He started shaking after he told me that he liked being taken care of.

Seeing him like that, so close to me but too far away to comfort, to touch, ignited a fire under my ass and I was by his side quicker than Superman getting changed in a phone booth. I had no idea what *that* was. But it was such a strong force that I didn't even question it.

His body pressed into mine and he steadied himself. His breathing returned to normal as mine sped up, fueled by the euphoria flooding my body, that I had been able to comfort him like that. In just the exact way that he needed, through instinctive touch.

For some reason, that settled my nerves. I was new to this whole Daddy/boy thing. Heck, even if there hadn't been an age difference between us, I sucked at talking in any kind of relationship. But the age gap did add a different dynamic to things.

It meant that I'd need to step up and talk, and no matter how hard it was, I was determined to push through it. I wanted to. I wanted to do it for me so that I could, at almost forty, finally get what I wanted. And I also wanted to do it for him. Mikey was making me feel things I'd never felt before. It was exciting, it was fun, and only just a little bit terrifying.

But what he said he wanted in a relationship wasn't actually that terrifying at all. It sounded completely reasonable. I don't think I would have been comfortable with a total twenty-four seven, heavily controlled Daddy/boy setup. It's great that it worked for some, but that just wasn't...me.

I wanted someone who could be himself, and could still surprise me. That was one thing I was certain about with Mikey —nonstop surprises. Whether he was just saying whatever was on his mind or kissing me so hungrily at a diner, it was all so...

"You're smiling," Mikey said with a cheeky gleam in his eyes. "What are you thinking about?"

"You," I replied instantly, and his body shuddered in response.

"Ooh, what about me?" he said, playfully swirling his spoon around in the bowl.

"I was thinking about what you said before. About relationships. And what you like." I could feel my heart racing, as if I was running a marathon, but I kept going. "And I, uh...I think that's what I would like too."

"What exactly did you like?" he said, bringing the spoon to his mouth and licking the whipped cream off seductively.

Oh, he was obviously doing that on purpose. No one eats a sundae like they're licking a...Oh god, my thoughts were going down a very inappropriate rabbit hole.

He flashed me an unconvincing, oh-so-innocent smile. He

knew what he was doing, alright. He was enjoying making me sweat, literally. I could feel beads of sweat cascading down my back like a waterfall.

"I like the balance that you talked about. I like the idea of you being independent and making your own decisions. But I also like that you'd lean on me and let me guide you. I like that you'd be..."

Oh no, I couldn't. I couldn't say it. It was too much. What if it freaked him out? That would freak *me* out and then we'd be two guys freaking out in a diner with a half-eaten sundae between us.

But I had to. I had to push through this. He was looking at me with those wide, baby blue eyes. I didn't know if he could tell there was a war raging inside of me, but if he could, he didn't say anything. He just looked at me, his head cocked to the side and his lips curled into a soft smile that seemed to say *just take your time*.

I scratched my arm as I finally worked up the courage to say it.

"I like that you'd be...mine."

It came out low and soft, so low that I wasn't sure he'd even heard it. It wasn't until a single tear rolled down his cheek that I knew he had.

Whatever that asshole ex of his had done to him had hurt the poor boy so badly. My heart ached for him. He placed his fingers in my hand and I gave them a hard squeeze.

"Thank you for talking, Stirling," he said with a genuine smile.

I didn't know what to say. No one had ever said that to me before, because I'd literally never talked to anyone like this. I picked up my spoon and dug into what was left of the sundae.

Mikey grabbed his spoon as well, and we sat there, eating our sundae in silence, holding hands across the table.

Holy shit, I'd done it. I'd actually done it. I had talked. And the world didn't blow up or anything. I felt a little unsteady. Sure, it had been a little weird, but a good kind of weird.

And then from nowhere, a massive yawn escaped from me.

"I'm sorry," I said, covering my mouth, trying to hide it.

"All this talking got you a little tired, huh?" Mikey said, but there wasn't any bite to his words.

"Just a big week," I admitted sheepishly.

"That's okay, I understand," he said, lightly grazing his fingers up my forearm. And fuck if that didn't feel amazing. "Did you want to talk about it? The court case, I mean?"

The all-too-familiar tightness in my throat returned and I looked at him blankly.

"It's okay if you don't want to," he said as his head drooped to the side.

"Some other time?" I asked, and he nodded. Thankfully.

I didn't want to ruin the evening. I had a tendency for doing that whenever I brought the case up. It was a major bummer and I didn't want to go there right then. And, okay, there may have been a little avoidance thrown in there too. But I would tell him eventually.

"Hey," I said, and he looked up.

"Can we do this again?" I asked once the server had cleared our table.

"What? Have dinner here with a side of therapy, you mean?" he asked with that devilishly cute smile of his.

"Well sure, but...I want to see you again. Can I see you again Mikey?"

"Hmm," he said, stroking his chin, his fingertips brushing against the lower lip I had tasted so recently. "I might have to check my diary. I'm awfully busy too, you know."

I smiled. "I'm sure you are. Think you can squeeze me in?"

He smiled back.

"Oh, I know I can squeeze you in." And with that, my cheeks burned hot and Mikey's sweet laugh rang out between us. "Oh, you're not all sweet and innocent are you, Mr. Bishop?"

His stare deepened. The heat from his eyes rushed to my cheeks, my neck, the warmth spreading through my body.

"No," he said, rubbing his hands slowly. "You're not Mr. Sweet and Innocent at all."

I pressed my palms into the table and leaned over toward him, his body mirroring my movement as he leaned in too.

In a hushed voice, I said, "Oh, Mikey...you have no idea. No idea at all."

CHAPTER ELEVEN

MIKEY

I was bleeding, the microwave was beeping at me, and I was running way behind schedule.

Shit, shit, shit.

The only positive was that my ass looked super fine in these jeans. Not exactly a surprise, but it was the only thing making me feel good as I ran into the bathroom to find a Band-Aid for the cut on my finger.

Maybe suggesting dinner at my place wasn't such a great idea after all. But seeing how tired Stirling had been on our date, and how much he had going on in his life, I'd figured a quiet evening in, with a romantic dinner by candlelight, was what he needed. That's what I wanted to do for him. That's what was blowing up in my face right now. Cooking was a lot harder than it looked on TV.

I found the Band-Aids in the bathroom, grabbed them, and raced back into the kitchen to find the water boiling over and the microwave still beeping incessantly at me. I threw the Band-Aids on the table, placed a tissue around my finger to keep the bleeding at bay, and turned the heat down to stop the water boiling over.

I rushed over to the microwave and opened it, stopping that incessant beeping noise at last. I touched the tip of the broccoli with my finger and it was still stone cold. How could that be? It didn't make any sense. I punched in twenty minutes and set the microwave off again. That should cook them through...I hoped.

The only thing that was working in the kitchen was the apple crumble that I had just placed in the oven. I smiled proudly. At least I could count on that to be a success. I quickly looked around the kitchen to make sure that I had thrown away the crumble's packaging as I wrapped a Band-Aid over my small cut.

My momentary reprieve was interrupted by the doorbell. I fished my phone out of my pocket. Seven o'clock, right on the dot. Of course he was the ridiculously punctual type. A small smile escaped my lips as I walked over to the door.

Opening it, my breath caught in my throat at the sight of the man standing on the other side. The simplicity of his outfit—a tight-fitting, long-sleeve black shirt that hugged his body in a way that made me jealous, faded blue jeans, and black boots—got my pulse racing. It highlighted his perfectly proportioned features beautifully. Broad shoulders, slim waist, muscular legs, and that solid, beefy ass of his that I wanted to knead like it was Play-Doh.

But there was no way I could miss the tiredness written all over him. He looked even more tired than he had the previous week at the diner. His face, while still handsome, looked drawn. His eyelids drooped heavily over his sagging eyes and the bright, piercing green of his eyes was lighter, faded.

It was all too much for my poor little brain, torn between the lust the sight of him elicited in me, and the genuine concern I felt for his wellbeing. So, of course, the first words I blurted out were, "You look like shit."

Immediately, his shoulders slumped a little and a dejected look stretched across his face.

He forced a smile.

"Well that's a lovely way to say hello."

He took a step toward me, handing me a bouquet of flowers that he'd hidden behind his back. I stepped in at the same time, a little too quickly, and stepped on his foot, causing him to lose his balance and slam into the doorframe.

"Oh my god, I'm so sorry," I cried out. "Are you okay?"

"Yeah, I'm fine," he said, as he steadied himself on his feet and rubbed down the side of his arm. "This must be a new record."

There was a fire lighting up his eyes, removing any signs of tiredness, as he grabbed me by the waist and pulled me in, the force of our bodies squashing the flowers between us.

"What—what do you mean?" I asked. It came out softer, more breathless than I wanted, but that's the effect he had on me, especially with his hands on my hips.

"In under sixty seconds, you've managed to insult me and physically hurt me," he said in a low, affectionate tone, gently tracing his thick fingers along my jaw. I let out a small sigh at the surprising softness of his touch.

I tilted my head back, closing my eyes as his warm lips met mine. His hand swooped around to the back of my neck, but he didn't pull me in closer, he just held me there. I melted into the warmth of his hand. His touch was more about presence, letting me know he was there, than trying to control my body.

His kiss was the same. Gentle. A little bit of presence, a whole lot of teasing.

We pulled our bodies apart, our eyes open and locked onto each other. The silence between us buzzed with electricity.

Then another something started to buzz. The microwave. Again. Shit.

Something that sounded like a bomb going off rang out as I raced to the warzone my kitchen had become.

"What is going on in there?" Stirling asked with concern rising in his voice.

He was one step behind me and I could feel his warm breath on the back of my neck, landing on the exact same spot where he'd had his hand pressed against me.

"I'm cooking, or at least trying to," I said over my shoulder as we stepped into the second round of my cooking nightmare.

Water was overflowing from the pot again, the oven was making all sorts of weird rattling noises, and that goddamn microwave was beeping like a motherfucker.

I let out a defeated sigh as I felt two capable hands on my shoulders, gently moving me aside. Stirling brushed past me and, in an instant, he transformed into a cooking superhero. He deftly turned off the stove and the oven, removed the pot with the overflowing water from the stovetop, and turned off the microwave. Finding a pair of oven mitts, he took the broccoli out and placed it on the counter.

His slow and steady demeanor had morphed into a quick-thinking, problem-solving machine. I was fascinated by how quickly he could move while his face remained calm. In the midst of all of the chaos, he was a steady presence.

With the kitchen brought under his control, he took a few steps toward me. His movement was back to its seductively slow pace as he dragged his eyes up and down my body.

"Remember that time you were worried I was going to kill you in the woods?" he began jokingly, as he pressed his index finger to my nose.

I tilted my head upward, transfixed by those deep green eyes of his that had come alive, probably due to all the kitchen commotion. Or maybe...because of me?

"Uh huh," I breathed.

"Well this," he said, pointing around my kitchen, "is a whole lot scarier."

"I don't really do a whole lot of cooking."

"Yeah," he said with a nod and a smile. "I figured as much."

I pulled myself away from him and looked around the kitchen. It was a mess. Dinner was ruined. Everything was ruined. My lower lip started to tremble as the enormity of my fuck-up hit me.

I'd ruined the whole night. All I'd wanted to do was cook him a nice meal, so that he could relax and unwind after a hard week, and I had messed everything up.

"I'm sorry I insulted you," I said, turning to him but unable to look him in the eyes. "I'm sorry I stepped on your foot and I'm sorry I've ruined dinner. I'm sorry I've ruined the whole evening."

"You haven't ruined anything." His voice was the perfect blend of calm, reassuring, and sexy as hell.

"I have. I said you look like shit. I ruined steak, potatoes, and vegetables, the easiest meal in the world. Who does that?"

A smile broke out on his face and I felt his finger gently lift my chin up, my eyes meeting his warm, inviting gaze.

"You do, Mikey. You do. And you know what?" he said as he moved in closer to me again, placing his hand on my arm. "That's what I like about you. You are who you are, and there's no one else in the world like you."

I smiled as I leaned into his hand, as reassured by his words as I was by his touch.

He fished out his phone from his pocket.

"So apparently these things can order food." I giggled. "You like Chinese?"

I nodded, and within half an hour, we had cleaned the kitchen up, the food had arrived, and we were sitting at the table enjoying our meal. At least I got the candles and the nice-table-setting part of the evening right.

Stirling's strong features flashed seductively in the candlelight. His tiredness disappeared in the dim light. I wanted to find out why he was always so tired. Was it this court case of his? So I asked him about it—again—and to my surprise, he told me.

"My mom and dad lived in a retirement community in Florida. They were in their seventies and did that thing where people move somewhere warmer," he started. "My father called me randomly one Wednesday night, saying that mom wasn't feeling well after having some chicken for dinner. I was concerned but, you know, I didn't think too much of it. It was one bad meal."

I nodded my head as he continued.

"When I called the next day to check in on her and she still wasn't better, I told her to call the retirement community's doctor for a home visit to find out what it was. She said they had tried but that no one had come."

"That's terrible," I said.

"It gets worse. When she was feeling even sicker on the Friday morning, and the doctor still hadn't shown up—despite both my father and I calling the medical team multiple times—I lost my shit. When the doctor finally did turn up, she was so pale and weak they had to take her into the hospital immediately. When I heard the news, I was panicked and jumped on the next available flight."

My mouth was dry. I knew this wasn't going to end well. I could see Stirling's chest heaving, the pain still raw.

"While I was on the flight down, she fell into a coma. I rushed straight from the airport to the hospital, but I was too late. She went from feeling unwell after dinner on Wednesday to being dead by Friday night."

"Oh my God, Stirling, I am so, so sorry." My voice was cracked and a lump had formed in my throat.

"The autopsy report confirmed that she'd had a reaction to the food. A reaction that, if acted upon and treated in time, could have been handled with medication and rest. But due to the retirement community's failure to respond to our repeated requests for treatment, she died. That's why I'm suing. She didn't deserve to die because of one bad meal."

From the way his voice softened every time he mentioned her, I could tell he still loved her dearly. It reminded me of the way I felt about my mom, who was my whole world and best friend, well, apart from Nick.

I was shocked to hear that he had been fighting for justice for his mom for that long—*three freaking years*—and that it still wasn't over yet. There was no way it should have taken all this time, and taken so much out of his life. I felt bad for him, and so hopeless at the same time, knowing there was nothing I could do to help make it better.

"Well, there you have it," he said when he was finished with the story. "That's my shitshow of a life in a nutshell."

And with that, he let out a massive yawn. It came out of nowhere and must have surprised him too, because he quickly scrambled to cover his mouth. I loved seeing him in those little unguarded moments.

"And I've become a terrible sleeper," he said by way of explanation.

The self-conscious look on his face made me want to leap across the table and wrap myself around him. Although, knowing my luck, my shirt would have caught the candle and started a fire, and my attempt at romance would have ended in disaster. One that would have probably involved first responders.

After we finished our meal, he got up and began clearing the table.

"Let me do that," I said, standing up and taking his plate from him. "I'll clean up and..."

I hesitated.

His eyes narrowed as he looked at me.

"What are you up to, Mikey?"

I collected all of the empty takeout containers on the table and turned to face him.

"Do you trust me?"

A smile stretched his thick lips as he looked up at me, recognizing that I was asking him the same question he'd asked me in his pickup truck on our first date.

"I do," he replied in that voice of his that always made my insides flip with happiness.

"I was going to wait a few more dates to do this...but you look so tired."

Believe it or not, I was trying to make up for my previous *foot-in-mouthness*. I hoped Stirling would see it that way too.

His smile let me know that he got my sense of humor.

"Back to throwing insults now, are we?" he said, the warmth shining through his words.

"I'll be right back," I said over my shoulder as I started toward the kitchen. "Keep your clothes on, but take off your shoes and socks."

The look of surprise on his face sent a hot thrill through me.

For a man who was always so calm and in control, I loved being able to surprise him.

I threw the containers into the bin and made my way down the short hallway to my bedroom. I glanced over at him. He'd left the table and walked over to the couch in the living room. I could see him taking off his socks and shoes, as instructed, slowly and steadily as always. I almost squealed in delight as I rushed into my bedroom to grab the two things I needed.

A few moments later, I was back in the living room standing in front of Stirling. He was barefoot and sitting on the couch, looking up at me with an adorably confused expression.

"What are you up to, Mikey Harrison?" he said in a low, devilish growl.

I pulled my hands from behind my back, showing him a bottle of oil in one hand, and a small, wooden foot stick in the other.

"This!" I said, and the confusion that danced across his handsome features was abso-fucking-lutely priceless.

CHAPTER TWELVE

STIRLING

"What the hell is that?"

"This," Mikey said, stretching out his hand with the short brown stick, "is a foot stick. And this is some body oil."

He waved the container toward me.

I must have been really tired because I still wasn't getting it.

"Okay..." I said slowly, as Mikey dropped to his knees and sat cross-legged on the floor in front of me.

"I'm a trained reflexologist, I'll have you know," he said with that familiar, harmless cockiness of his.

"Really?" It came out higher pitched than I had intended, as I adjusted myself on the sofa to get a better view of him.

"Well, Nick and I did a weekend course once. So I guess that makes us trained, right?"

I let out a big laugh.

"Sure it does," I said as Mikey lifted my left foot and placed it on his lap.

"I'm going to give you a foot rub to help ease off some of that tension, and maybe even some of that tiredness," he said, looking up at me through his dark lashes.

God, he really knew how to get me all worked up. Just the sight of him on the floor, staring at me with those big blue eyes of his and that innocent—yet not innocent at all— expression on his face. I nodded and grumbled something that I hoped was at least semi-coherent.

Mikey was full of surprises. I wasn't usually someone who liked surprises. I preferred to know things in advance so that I could prepare for them. But with Mikey, it was different. It wasn't scary or unpleasant. In fact, it was the exact opposite. It was exciting and fun.

Even if he did accidentally insult me, or bump into me, or almost blow his kitchen up. His lack of filter and propensity for clumsiness only added to his appeal.

They were what made Mikey, Mikey.

They also made it easier for me to open up and talk to him. I had been avoiding talking about the court case with him, simply because it had invaded every other aspect of my life already. I didn't want it coming into this relationship too.

But he had asked about it a number of times, and I had seen the look of disappointment when I hadn't wanted to talk about it at the diner. I figured I just had to do it and get it done. He wanted to know and he had a right to. It was the main reason why I was always so tired.

I told him about it over dinner and it felt...fine. More than fine, actually. It felt like a relief, like a small part of the burden was lifted because I had shared it with him.

I wondered if that was what it would feel like when I opened up to him about what I wanted when it came to sex. Would it be freeing? Would it be a relief, an unburdening of sorts? There was only one way to find out for sure.

"This takes me back," I said, smiling as Mikey rubbed some of the oil onto his hands.

"What? Even though I'm not practically naked and you're not using me as a piece of human furniture?"

I winced at his smart-ass reply and he burst out laughing at my reaction, the sound warm and enticing.

He lifted my left foot slightly and rubbed oil up and down the entire underside of it. Even this, the gentle pressure of his rubbing, felt incredible. With his thumb, he pressed into the fleshy part of my sole, starting at my heel and gently dragging it up to my toes.

"Fuuuuuck, that feels amazing," I said.

My eyelids fluttered shut and my head fell back as I allowed myself to fall into the pleasure of the feeling.

"Not too hard?" he asked.

"No... It's... Perfect."

And it was. He kept rubbing, applying the most exquisite amount of pressure and my whole body was responding, the long-built-up tension seeping out of me. I opened my eyes and stared at the ceiling, my head rocking gently in response to his movements.

"So, what are you into when it comes to sex?"

The words pulled my head down to look at him with such force, I thought I'd given myself whiplash. He was just sitting there, ever so calmly, massaging my feet. As if he hadn't just asked the hardest question in the world to answer.

"I, uh..."

I tapped my fingers nervously on the sofa. How the fuck was I meant to answer this one? I mean, I'd done well and had opened up to him—a lot—but this was something else entirely. How did I tell him what I wanted sexually?

As luck would have it, I wouldn't have to...at least not yet.

"Would it help you if I told you what I was into?" he asked, and I let out a massive exhalation.

"Yes," I replied, still feeling the oppressive tightness in my throat. "If you don't mind, that is."

Now it was Mikey's turn to look all sorts of anxious. He gently let go of my foot. I tried to move it, but he kept it there, snug against his lap. He put the foot stick down and looked up at me, his wide eyes filled with uncertainty.

"It's taken me a long time to figure this out about myself." His voice was faint, almost timid, but there was a steeliness in his eyes as well.

"For the longest time, something just didn't feel right for me when it came to sex. I just didn't know what it was."

I wasn't sure what he was talking about specifically, but I nodded anyway, letting him take all the time he needed. I knew how awful it was to feel rushed or pressured to talk. Whatever he was about to say was obviously a big deal for him, and I wanted to respect that.

"I've always had a high sex drive, but I was never into anything, you know?"

"What do you mean *into anything*?" I asked, keeping my tone measured.

"Well, you know. Some guys are into leather, or role playing, or just plain old vanilla sex...whatever it is. I've—I've never had that pull toward any one thing when it came to sex."

"Okay..."

"Which made me feel like something was wrong with me, like something was missing. But then I realized what I was into, what I actually really wanted more than anything else in the world, which is..."

He stopped himself and I could see his hand starting to tremble.

I wanted to reach down and bring him up right beside me,

hold him tight in my arms. But I needed to give him space. He was strong, and I knew he could get through this. I could tell that he wanted to.

"Yes..."

"I want to please and I want to serve."

He looked away, his eyes downcast on the floor. I thought he was finished, but he looked up again and continued.

"I don't really mind what the thing is. Whether it's BDSM or if you're into cuddling, or blowjobs, or fucking me with the lights out, or fucking me with the lights on and the curtains open, whatever you're into sexually...me pleasing and serving you is what gets me off more than anything else—within reasonable limits, of course."

He let out a deep breath, one he'd been holding on to for a while.

My mouth fell open. If I usually had trouble finding the words to say, now I didn't even know where to begin to look for them.

I looked at him, sitting on the floor, with my feet in his lap, and he looked scared, vulnerable, alone. A deep longing unfurled in my heart and took over my body. I wanted him beside me. No, I *needed* him beside me. I needed to touch and hold him, caress his skin, brush his hair off his forehead, feel his breath on me.

"Is—is that...okay?" The words floated from his lips and struck me in the chest.

Was it okay? It was more than okay, it was...everything I wanted too. So why couldn't I say it? Why was it so fucking hard to just say it?

"You have no idea how much what you just said means to me."

I let out a massive breath and slumped back into my chair. They were nice words, good words, but I was frustrated at myself. They weren't the words I wanted to say, the words that were burning in my chest, begging to be spoken.

"Thank fuck for that," Mikey said as he let out a massive sigh. "You have no idea how hard you are to read sometimes."

He picked up my right foot, applied oil to it, and began pressing his fingers firmly.

I squirmed as the pressure jolted into all the tight spots in my body. All five million of them. I was so stressed and so tightly wound.

"Just breathe," Mikey said. "It's easier if you breathe. Your body will start to relax."

"Oh, okay," I said.

I took a deep breath. He was right. The pressure was still firm, but the harsh sting had lessened. My eyelids grew heavy as my breathing slowed, deepening with each breath in and each breath out. In and out...

"You like this?" Mikey's voice gently stirred me back to life.

How much time had passed? I had no idea. I kept my eyes closed and simply moaned to signal my happiness.

"Yeah, I can uh, kinda tell."

What? I opened my eyes and swung my head downward toward Mikey and...the massive tent pole that had formed in my pants.

"Oh shit! I'm sorry," I said, shuffling my legs backward and pressing a palm over my crotch to flatten the hardness.

Mikey's sweet laugh filled the air. "That's okay. But if you want to apologize about anything, maybe it should be your snoring?"

"I fell asleep? I was snoring?" I asked, completely mortified as heat crept up my neck.

Mikey kept laughing and nodding his head.

"It's okay though," he said. "It was more of a purr than a snore. I actually kinda liked it."

I was embarrassed, but the blissful state I was in blunted its impact.

"You're tired. It's okay," he continued with a genuine softness in his bright eyes. "Besides, can I just say that the view from down here is mighty impressive? *Mighty* impressive."

I chuckled and loosened my shoulders to relax myself a little. Then I stopped abruptly and looked down at myself, realizing he was talking about my hard-on, which was becoming the hardest hard-on ever.

I was almost forty, why the hell wasn't it going down? But nope, it just stood there defiantly, belligerently teasing me with its presence, protruding proudly from my body, massively tenting my pants and refusing all of my reasonable mental pleas for it to go down.

"Why don't you...touch it?" Mikey's voice rumbled lower than I had ever heard.

He looked up at me. His smile was wicked. His blue eyes sparkled in mischievous delight.

"You want me to...?" I finished the rest of that question with the motion of my hands.

"Yes." There was a breathy urgency in his voice as the heat between our bodies increased. He may have been sitting away from me, but we were connected by the pressure he was still applying to my feet, stroking them up and down, sending waves of pleasure throughout my entire body.

Including my cock, which seemed to be *especially* responsive.

I kept my eyes glued to Mikey's as I loosened my belt buckle and undid the buttons on my fly. I shuffled and pulled my pants halfway down my legs to just above my knees. My cock was straining against my briefs. Mikey noticed the wet patch at the top of my briefs at the same time I did, and the way he licked his lips made my cock pulsate in approval. Okay, now it was just showing off.

"You want me to take these off?" I asked him, deciding that Mikey wasn't the only one who could tease and torment. He nodded his head in short little bursts, his eyes burning into my bulge and his tongue firmly planted in the corner of his mouth.

"What do you say?" I teased, and his eyes lit up like fireworks as he caught on to what I was doing.

"Show me your cock, please...*Daddy.*"

My cock thickened, swelling in response to his words, the last word in particular. The way it oozed out of his delicious lips. The way it filled the air between us with an undeniable electric charge. My body felt tingly all over, a feeling I had never felt before.

I hooked the waistband of my briefs with my thumbs. Slowly —painfully and deliberately slowly—I began to drag my underwear down the hard length of my cock, inch by inch, watching Mikey's eyes dance with anticipation.

Finally, as I pulled the briefs over my swollen head, my rock-hard cock, now freed, slapped back onto my belly with a heavy, filthy-sounding smack. A second later, a tender gasp escaped from Mikey's mouth.

"You've—you've got a nice cock." His deliberately controlled tone didn't match the heat smoldering in his look.

He may have started this, but I wasn't done teasing the boy yet. I was enjoying seeing him like this. Excited. Anticipating. Raw.

"Oh yeah," I said, as I ran my thumb from the base all the way up to the head of my cock. I slid my thumb across the slit, scooping up a thick, pearly drop of release. I stretched my fingers out toward Mikey and he instantly leaned in closer, gently opening his mouth.

I pulled back, and slowly brought my thumb to my mouth. I

guessed he wouldn't like what would happen next and I was right.

His eyebrows arched in surprise and his lips formed a tight pout as he realized he would be deprived. This time, at least. His eyes stared hungrily at my hand as I ran my thumb over my tongue, feeding the thick, salty release to myself, my eyes glued to his.

His look of disappointment was quickly replaced with something else...animalistic lust. I may have won the round, but the battle was far from over, and Mikey wasn't wasting any time making the next move.

He wiped his hands on a small towel and began to trace his fingers up my legs. The friction of his fingertips against my leg hairs relaxed and excited me at the same time.

I looked down and saw his long, slender fingers wrap around the base of my cock. He squeezed it, harder than I thought he would, and it sent a bolt of heat up my spine.

He ran his fingers up and down my length, looking at me with those deep blue eyes the whole time. With his gaze still fixed to mine, he opened his mouth and slapped the head of my now inflamed, purple cockhead against his warm, wet tongue.

When I next looked down, he was taking my cock in his mouth. This time, he was the one being slow and deliberate. Oh, the cheeky boy. He looked up at me and chuckled, the vibration bubbling up his throat, coating my cock with the most amazing warm sensation. My fingers dug into the sofa and I bucked my hips into the pleasure.

His mouth widened as he made his way down my cock with a sultry determination.

"Mikey, it's okay if you can't take it all...Oh, fuuuuck..."

My head fell back as his nose hit my pubic bone, taking me, taking all of me, inside his mouth. His warm, wet mouth enveloped me like a plush blanket.

"That feels incredible, Mikey."

He drew down the length of me and looked up, his face alive with desire. His pace, his pressure, everything was perfect. I sank deeper into the pleasure, gently wrapping my fingers around the back of his head. His soft, guttural moan told me he liked that.

Not that he needed me to apply any pressure. Gone was Mr. Slow and Steady and in his place was Mr. Fast and Furious. He began to suck me with a seriousness that caught me by surprise, but felt incredible.

"Yeah Mikey, that's it," I panted as I felt my balls tightening. "That feels so good."

My hands around his head, my cock deep in his throat. The sounds of him sucking me hungrily, filling the room.

Until I heard the door opening. Then, footsteps. Then, oh my fucking God...

I pushed Mikey aside as quickly and carefully as I could. I scrambled to stand up, my hands diving for my pants, desperately yanking them up my thighs.

Mikey's confused face looked up at me as I tried to stand up.

"I'm sorry, officer. I had no idea. I swear he told me he was..."

I took a step forward, forgetting my feet were slicked in oil. I immediately lost my balance and fell back onto the couch in one undignified swoop. My pants caught around my legs, my legs swung over my head, and there I was, exposing my bare ass to one very unamused police officer.

And then...bursts of laughter assaulted my ears as I fumbled around, trying to sit myself up, my pants wrapped in frustratingly stubborn knots around my legs. I looked over at Mikey, who was rolling on the floor howling with laughter, tears streaming down his face.

"I'm sorry, I'm sorry, I shouldn't be laughing but..."

What the hell was happening here? Why was there a cop in Mikey's living room? Why was Mikey laughing like he'd just seen the funniest thing ever? Why the fuck were my pants tied in a freaking knot?

I looked back over at the cop who looked just as confused as I was, his eyes darting between Mikey and me.

"Are you going to arrest me?" I asked, because...what the hell else was I going to say to a cop?

"Why would I arrest you for dating my brother?" he replied.

"Your brother?" I looked over at Mikey who had finally, *finally* managed to regain some composure, enough for him to sit upright and speak, at least.

"Stirling, meet my brother, Ben. Ben, this is the guy I was telling you about."

"Oh, hey, Stirling, nice to meet you," Ben said completely casually, as if a simple introduction was all that was needed here. Meanwhile, I was still lying on my back with half of my ass hanging out.

Mikey grabbed a towel and began wiping the oil off my feet while my brain continued to play catch-up.

"You live with your brother?"

"Yep," Mikey said. "I told you that, remember? And I told you that he's a cop."

"Shit, you did. I'm sorry, Mikey. I must have forgotten."

"I might leave you guys to it. Nice to meet you, Stirling." And with that, Ben turned around, and a few moments later I heard a bedroom door close.

Mikey kept scrubbing the towel against the soles of my feet.

"God, I really lathered it on thick. It's kinda hard to get this off. Sorry, this might take a minute."

I fell back and closed my eyes. I was mortified. I was beyond embarrassed. And...I was happier than I had been in years.

At that moment, with Mikey manically trying to scrub the excess oil off my feet, with me having survived an evening of unintended insults, physical injuries, and a myriad of near-miss accidents in the kitchen, with having received the most amazing blowjob I'd ever gotten in my life, and with it all ending with me tripping and falling over to expose my bare butt to his brother—I realized something.

I was falling in love with Mikey Harrison.

CHAPTER THIRTEEN

MIKEY

"Well, I certainly look forward to meeting him. From what I've heard, he's got a wonderful ass."

"Ma," I cried out.

Not exactly the words I was expecting to hear from my mom, but I wasn't *that* surprised, either. In some ways, it made telling her about Stirling easier. She already had my brother vouching for him...or his ass, at least.

I'd perched myself on a stool at the breakfast bar in the small, cozy kitchen, and as I brought the glass of red wine to my lips, I asked, "When did Ben tell you?"

"He called this morning," she said as she dipped her fingers into the sauce bubbling away on the stove top. She smacked her lips together heavily, her head gently swaying as if summoning the taste gods for divine inspiration. "More oregano," she said with a firm nod.

The taste gods had spoken.

"He said it was very big, very muscly. Does he do a lot of squats like Nick does? I heard they make your booty pop."

Okay, now *those* were words I wasn't expecting to hear coming out of my mother's half-American, half-Italian mouth.

"Ma," I exclaimed with a laugh, putting the wine down on the counter and looking at the woman standing in front of me.

Her short dark hair was brushed to the side, tucked in behind her ear, she was wearing her favorite apron covered in years of light stains that not even the strongest detergent could remove. Her wide eyes were darting around, keeping tight control over the meal she was making.

"Don't you 'ma' me," she said, wagging a wooden spoon playfully at me. "A fine ass is a good thing to have."

I couldn't argue with that. I nodded, taking another sip of wine while making a mental note to keep Nick away from my mother for a while. Who else would she have gotten *booty pop* from?

Despite having lived in the states since her mid-twenties, and speaking English fluently, mom's accent was laced with that unmissable Italian sass, which came out in force when she went into full-on mom mode.

She was the best mom in the world, but I did worry about her living alone. She was in her early fifties and was still so young, but like she always said, she'd had her true love and that was enough for her.

Ma met Dad one summer when he was travelling in Italy while he was still in college. They had both gotten jobs in a winery in a little village in southern Italy, squashing the grapes with their feet that old-fashioned, traditional way.

With a backdrop like that—making wine by day, drinking wine by night—how could they not have fallen madly in love with one another? They tried the long-distance thing for a while but it didn't work, so she moved to the US in her mid-twenties.

Ben was born a year later, and I came two years after him. My childhood was filled with nothing but happy memories. We were a typical close-knit family. We'd spend the holidays surrounded by a huge gathering of all the immediate and extended family members. Between them, Mom and Dad had a football team of siblings, so there were always uncles, aunties, and countless cousins to catch up with.

Summers would be spent by the sea or travelling back to Italy, where again, life revolved around family. And pasta. And from when I was fifteen onward, with wine. Good, rich, full-bodied red wine.

Life was pretty damn perfect until a car crash killed my father as he was driving into work one morning. I was ten, and from that moment on, Mom went into full-on mama bear mode, looking after, protecting, and loving Ben and me enough for two parents.

But we were adults now, or at least trying to be. We were grown up and getting on with our lives. But fourteen years later, Ma was still single. It didn't feel right, somehow. She deserved another chance at happiness. If not a husband or boyfriend—and since booty calls were definitely out of the question—at least a companion. Preferably one with a fine ass.

"Now where did I put the...ah, here it is," she said, reaching for the wooden spoon as she stirred the oregano into the bubbling red bolognese sauce.

"I'll set the table," I said, getting up.

"Thanks darling. Dinner is almost ready."

Our weekly dinners were the highlight of my week. Usually Ben came along too, but that night he'd been called into the station at the last minute. I grabbed some plates and cutlery, moving around the kitchen with an ease that I was clearly lacking in my own.

This was the house that I grew up in, I knew every nook and

cranny of it like the back of my hand. The familiarity of it all—
Ma and Ben, our weekly dinners, this house—were the steadying
anchor at times when everything else in my life was going to shit.
The place that I could return to when I felt lost, the place that
reminded me of who I was.

A few moments later, we were both seated at the dinner
table about to enjoy, or in my case devour, a plateful of Nonna's
secret recipe spaghetti bolognese.

"This smells great, Ma, thanks," I said, shovelling in my first
mouthful of the thick, made-by-her-own-hand pasta.

Mom looked at me and smiled. Her eyes crinkling around
the edges, her smile lasting longer than usual before she glanced
around the table, looking almost a little lost, then picking up her
fork and spoon. She glanced over at me once more before she
started eating too.

"So tell me more about this man. I like his name. Stirling."

"So do I, Ma," I said, carefully slurping up a particularly
long strand of pasta.

I should have known better than to wear a white t-shirt to
dinner since I usually ended up with splotches of sauce all over
myself and my clothes.

If only she knew how much I liked the name. How much I
couldn't wait to be yelling it out at the top of my lungs....no wait,
this was neither the time nor the place to be jumping down that
sexual rabbit hole. My mom and I were very comfortable around
each other, I could pretty much tell her anything, but I didn't tell
her *everything*.

"Is he a good man?" she asked.

Good was her standard of character, the yardstick by which
she measured a person. It wasn't a judgemental *good-versus-bad*
kinda thing, it was more about whether they were of decent
character. A decent person who did decent things and avoided

the shitty, crappy things people could do to each other—steal, lie, betray, abuse.

It was her indirect way of asking, *Is he different from the others?*

"He is a very good person," I said, putting my fork and spoon down for a moment. "He won't hurt me."

It felt good to say those words, but it felt even better knowing they were true.

"Have you heard back from the college, Mikey? It's been a while now since you sat the entrance exam. Why haven't they gotten back to you?"

I barreled a bunch of pasta into my mouth, hoping the food would buy me some time, although there was no way to avoid it. Why had I told everyone about the course before I had even been accepted?

I'd gotten the email last week, the rejection email that told me I hadn't passed the entrance exam. I hadn't told her or Ben, hoping they'd forget. But she remembered—*of course* she remembered—and now here I was, faced with having to tell her that her youngest son was so fucking stupid that he couldn't even get into a program to study childcare. I mean, it wasn't like the bar was set particularly high for the program, and yet, I had still somehow managed to not get accepted.

Her light brown eyes narrowed in on me. She knew full well what I was doing, and like all good, slightly overprotective mothers, she wasn't having any of it.

"Mikey...what's wrong? What aren't you telling me?"

I swallowed my food, the last line of my defence. There was no way out. I was kinda surprised I'd been able to delay the inevitability of this moment for so long.

"I didn't get in, Ma," I said, wiping the napkin across the corners of my mouth. My voice was flat, dejected.

"When did you find out?"

Her eyebrow arched and her steely gaze felt like it could see right through me. I reached for backup, wine.

"Last week," I said, trying to hide behind the wine glass.

"Mikey, darling..." Her voice had softened, as had her eyes. "Why didn't you tell me before?"

"Because I felt like an idiot, Ma. I mean, who doesn't get in to study childcare? *Childcare.* I'm literally too dumb to play with kids and teach them the ABCs."

"Baby, you are not too dumb. Please don't speak like that," she said, her voice coated with love and concern. "You're a strong boy. Man," she corrected herself, although technically she'd been right the first time. "And you're not a quitter. Neither of my boys are. Your pa and I didn't raise you to just give up. When are you reapplying?"

"I'm—I'm not," I stammered and reached for more wine, preparing for the onslaught to come.

"*Mi-ke-leh,*" she said, her eyes lighting up with fire. Uh-oh. It was never good when she used my Italian name. "Why not? Why aren't you applying again?"

"I, uh..."

"Has something changed, do you want to study something else?"

"What? No..."

"Do you still want to work with children?"

"Yes, but..."

"Well then, what is your excuse for quitting? Tell me. Tell me right now."

I sighed. I had no excuse. I mean, I'd tried and failed once already. I could try and fail once more. Or maybe, I could try and not fail next time. No, I didn't want to get my hopes up again prematurely. That was the mistake I'd made last time. That was how I ended up under the fiery glare of my mother.

"I'll...think about reapplying, okay?"

That seemed to satisfy her, momentarily at least. Her face softened as she bit into her food.

"Please do, Mikey. Think about it. You're still so young. You still have your..."

Her eyes became unfocused and her body started to sway a little.

"Ma? You okay, Mom?" I asked, my jaw tightening with worry.

And then, just like that, she snapped back out of whatever that had been and said, "You still have your whole life ahead of you."

Her words were tinged with sadness.

We returned to a lighter conversation for the rest of the meal, which included the second helping I couldn't resist. Carbs were a rarity for me, so when I did indulge, I indulged big time. I put my carb-fueled energy to good use, though, clearing the table and putting the dirty dishes into the dishwasher while Mom settled in the living room.

When I returned, she was sitting on the floor, slowly thumbing through a black leather-bound photo album.

"What are you doing, Ma?" I asked, sitting down beside her.

I looked over and saw her face flooded with memories, her lips set in a permanent smile.

"Just...reminiscing. It's good to look back and remember the old times."

"Oh god," I said with a mortified giggle, pointing to a photo in the top right corner. "Look at my hair there. Why did you insist on giving us those silly bowl cuts?"

"I liked them. You boys looked so cute."

"Thank god you stopped giving us haircuts at home before we started school. That would have been so embarrassing."

"The only reason I stopped," she said, nudging me gently, the faint smell of her flowery perfume filling my nose, "was because I couldn't control a certain little someone. You had so much energy. Both of you did, actually."

"Yeah, I can imagine we were a handful," I chuckled.

"But," she said, cupping my face in her soft hands, "I wouldn't have had it any other way."

She gave me a quick kiss on my forehead before turning the page.

"Oh, look at you here, Mikey," she said as she tapped her finger gently over the photo. "You looked so adorable. I remember buying you those sandals. You basically had a fit the first time I tried to put them on you."

"Yeah, Ma, probably because even my four-year-old self could see how ugly they were," I joked, but then I looked closer at the photo. "Uh, Ma. Hang on, that's not me in the photo. That's Ben."

"Oh, is it?" she said and quickly turned the page. A little too quickly.

I looked at her and she seemed fine, she looked normal, but something was out of place. An uneasy feeling settled in the pit of my stomach, so I asked, "Ma...is anything wrong?"

She should have turned to me and said that she was fine. We should have spent the rest of the evening looking at old photos, laughing and reminiscing while eating one too many bowls of ice cream. It should have been like every other dinner, every other week.

But she didn't say she was fine.

When she turned to me, the look she gave sent a cold shiver through me. Her eyes were filled with worry and something I couldn't place, something I had never seen before.

She placed her hand gently over mine and said, "Mikey, darling, I don't want you to worry..."

Uh-oh...

"But I've been getting some tests done with a neurologist..."

Oh shit...

"And they've discovered something." She took a breath, steadying herself, her eyes starting to get misty around the edges. "I have early onset dementia."

No...no, no, no!

A heavy wave of panic crashed into my body. I was confused.

"How can you have dementia?" I asked. "You're only fifty. Isn't that something old people get?"

She brushed a strand of hair away that had fallen across my forehead.

"I'm fifty-three, darling, and yes, that is young. That's why it's called *early* onset dementia, Mikey. In a way, it's good they caught it so quick. It means there's a good chance to..."

"Cure it?" I asked hopefully.

Yes, that was it. That was how these things worked, wasn't it? The sooner you found a disease, the better the chances were to fully recover from it. I could feel the hope rising in my chest.

Please, please, *please* make that be the case here.

"Darling, there is no cure for dementia." Her words crushed my hope like water thrown on a fire. "But you can manage it."

"Manage it, how?" I asked.

I listened as she told me all about making lifestyle changes, eating certain foods and getting more exercise, but my eyes glazed over and I tuned her out.

All I knew was that my mom was sick, there was no cure, and things would never be the same again.

CHAPTER FOURTEEN

STIRLING

My phone vibrated loudly on the bedside table near my head. I clumsily fumbled around until my fingers found it, the screen lighting up the whole room. It was eleven and I had been asleep. With one bleary eye open, I looked at the screen. It was a text. From Mikey.

Mikey: *Are you awake?*

I quickly typed back, rubbing the sleep out of my eyes.

Me: *Yes.*
Me: *Are you okay?*

I knew something wasn't right.

Mikey: *No. I know it's late, but can you come pick me up?*
Mikey: *Please?*

I was dressed and in my truck, headed for Mikey's apartment, less than five minutes later.

He hadn't told me what was wrong, only that he wasn't hurt or in any immediate danger. While I was relieved about that, it didn't ease my nerves, knowing that something had upset him like this. Whatever it was, it was important enough for him to reach out this late. I tapped my fingers impatiently on the steering wheel. I didn't like not knowing.

I pulled up and Mikey was already waiting in front of his building, his arms wrapped around himself. He got in, his tear-soaked face shining in the moonlight.

"Mikey," I said, placing my hand around the back of his neck. I could feel him trembling under my palm. "What's wrong? What's happened?"

"Ben's working overnight and I don't want to be alone," he said, fighting against the tears that had started falling down his cheeks. "Can I..." he looked up at me, his blue eyes delicate and fragile. "Can I spend some time with you tonight?"

His voice was barely more than a whisper.

I nodded.

"Of course," I replied. "Do you need anything? Food? Or something to drink?"

"No, I'm okay," he said, wiping the tears from his face with the back of his hand. He looked up at me, struggling to keep control of his face. He swallowed and said, "I just want to be with you, Stirling."

Under normal circumstances, the words would have filled my heart with joy. But my concern for Mikey was overriding anything else I might have been feeling.

After a few minutes of driving in silence, glancing over every few seconds to make sure he was okay, Mikey started talking. He told me about his mom and finding out about her diagnosis earlier that evening.

Since arriving home, he'd been texting Ben, who had only found out about it earlier that afternoon. Nick was also at work, so Mikey couldn't talk to his best friend about it.

He was clearly in shock, and not having anyone beside him, the poor guy had worked himself up into a frenzy.

Not that I blamed him one bit. I could still remember the overwhelming panic I'd felt when I heard that my mom had been taken to the hospital. It had been the scariest feeling in the world, not knowing what would happen to her. I imagined Mikey would be going through the same sort of thing, especially given how close he was to his mom.

I placed my hand gently on his lap, and after a few moments, his shaking gradually subsided. He kept talking, but his pace slowed. By the time we pulled up at my house, he had calmed down a lot. Enough, anyway, for him to start taking everything in. It was his first time seeing where I lived.

As we stepped through the front door, his eyes darted around the place. It wasn't much, but it did the job. It was a modest three-bedroom house with a decent-sized backyard and a front porch. It was definitely a renovator's delight, but aside from doing the work that needed to be done when I had first moved in, I hadn't gotten around to really fixing the place up.

"I like your house," Mikey said.

He followed me past the living room and into the small kitchen at the back of the house.

"Thanks. Are you sure you're not hungry? I can make you a sandwich, or maybe you'd like some tea? Coffee?"

The image of him standing outside his apartment flashed through my mind. He looked so scared, so alone. Seeing him like that did something to me, it unlocked my protective side. I needed to look after him. I needed to do whatever it took to make him feel better.

"What's this?" he asked as he stepped over to the wall near the fridge.

"It's a calendar," I said. "You hang them on your wall so that you know what day it is."

"You need to be reminded of that, do you?" he smiled, and it was the first time I'd seen him relax a little since I'd picked him up.

I felt a sense of relief, despite his teasing.

"Stirling."

Mikey had closed the distance between us and was now standing close to me. Dangerously close to me.

He ran his fingers up my forearm. The drag of his fingertips against my skin, the deep gleam shining in his eyes, it was all an invitation.

An invitation I would have to decline.

"Mikey," I said, catching his hand in mine before it could go any farther. "What are you doing?"

"I just want to feel better. Can you help me feel better...Stirling?"

The forefinger of his other hand was gently tugging the front of my shirt. He wasn't making this easy for me.

I grabbed *that* hand and now, with both of his hands safely wrapped up in mine, I leaned in toward him and said, "Mikey, you've had some very bad news tonight. You're in shock. You're processing. I don't think we should do anything. I don't want to take advantage of you."

I meant it too. As much as I did want to have sex with him, I still hadn't talked to him, not properly, not about sex. And definitely not about what I was...into.

A dark look flashed across his face, replaced just as quickly by the sexiest smile I had ever seen.

"What makes you think you're taking advantage of me?" he asked, batting his eyelashes.

I smiled. "Nice try."

"I'm serious, Stirling."

"So am I," I said, gripping his hands a little tighter.

The naughty boy was trying to wriggle his way out of my grip, distracting me with tempting smiles and fluttering eyelids.

"Look, it's getting late," I said. "I can drive you back...or you can stay here tonight. I'll sleep in the guest room."

"No." His tone was definitive. I just wasn't sure which part he was saying no to. He must have seen the confused look on my face. His voice softened. "I mean, yes I'd like to stay, but no to you sleeping in the guest room."

Somehow, he'd managed to wrestle a hand free and slip it under my shirt. His nimble fingers grazed across my lower abdomen. My heart raced and my stomach flipped. Damnit. This was just what he wanted. I opened my mouth to say something.

"Shhh."

His other hand had somehow freed itself too, and he pressed my lips shut with his index finger. I should have been angry at him, or at least pretended to be, but it was taking all the strength I had not to open my mouth and lick those sweet fingers of his, taking them into my mouth and tasting him.

"Do you want me to be your boy, Stirling Bishop?"

I was suddenly finding it very hard to breath. Or speak. He released his finger from my lips and I instantly missed it.

"Yes." My voice was low, but my hunger was rising.

"Then say it."

Right. My turn to speak. Breathe.

"I want you to be my boy, Mikey Harrison."

"Good," he said. "And for that, you get a little reward."

He traced his tongue over my bottom lip, wetting it ever so

slightly, and then he pulled away. Leaving me wanting so much more.

"And do you want to be my Daddy, Stirling? Are you *ready* to be my Daddy?"

"Yes. I want to be your Daddy."

Saying the words felt good. I did, I fucking did.

"Good," Mikey replied.

"Now, where's my reward?"

I was getting some serious hunger pangs.

"Oh, you'll get your reward soon enough," he said as a wicked smile tugged at the corner of his lips.

Part of me couldn't believe the change—no, the *transformation*—in Mikey. Gone were the tears and trembling from when I had picked him up earlier. Here was this strong, seductive boy standing before me.

A boy who knew exactly what he wanted.

A boy who was going after—and getting—exactly what he wanted.

That's when I realized the mistake I had made. His tears weren't a weakness. They were his way of expressing himself and what he felt in that moment. Just like he was expressing himself and what he was feeling, wanting, and needing, in this moment.

A white-hot desire for him tore through my entire body. I'd never wanted anyone more than I wanted him. I grabbed his hand from under my shirt.

"Let's go," I said as I led him down the hallway to my bedroom.

The moment we entered the room, we morphed into a tornado of arms, lips, clothes falling off bodies, and feet being tripped over until we were both naked, the tips of our hard, warm cocks touching.

"Wait, wait, wait," I said, pulling away from his lips. They were bright red and slightly puffy, his porcelain skin flushed. "I, um, I don't have any protection."

"I was tested two months ago and I haven't been with anyone since. Except for you on my couch, but as I'm sure you remember, that didn't exactly end as expected."

A warm blush filled my cheeks at the memory. I had a feeling I was never going to live that down.

"No, it didn't. Well I got tested after Richard chea—left me. I was clean then, so..."

"Wait, wasn't that like, almost a year ago?" Mikey cut me off.

"Yeah," I said, looking straight at him. I could feel the vulnerability spilling out of me, but he was there, right there in front of me to catch me.

"You mean, you haven't..."

I shook my head and turned away. Shame flooded my body. Mikey placed his fingers gently under my chin, and I looked at him. There was no judgement on his face, just understanding.

"Guess you were just waiting for something good to come along."

Fuck, if his cheeky confidence didn't send a bolt of heat straight to the tip of my cock. He looked down at the movement and smiled. But I wasn't finished yet.

"I've only actually ever slept with three guys and they've all been, you know, boyfriends."

"Well," Mikey grabbed the sides of my face and looked at me with wide, expectant eyes, "make me your boyfriend."

The familiar word-choking sensation filled my throat.

"Mikey, will you be my..."

Before I could finish, Mikey's lips crashed into mine, his tongue ravenously exploring the insides of my mouth. I guessed that was my answer right there.

It took me a moment to find my footing, but when I did, I lifted him up into my arms. He wrapped his legs around my waist as I carried him over to the bed. I placed him down gently and took a step back, allowing myself to soak him in. His body was lean and smooth, his cock perfectly proportioned to the rest of him. His smile was tantalizingly inviting, like a deep, blue pool on a hot summer's day.

"I hope you're ready, boy, because I am going to devour you," I said as I lay my body over his, my hands beginning their slow exploration of every inch of his tight body.

"Show me what you got, Daddy. I hope I've been worth the wait."

"Oh you have, my beautiful boy. You have definitely been worth waiting for."

And with that, I was done with the *using words* portion of the evening.

I explored every inch of Mikey's body with my lips, my tongue, my fingers and hands. I wanted to discover everything there was to know. Where he liked to be touched, where his body was most responsive. I wanted to find and mentally map all the spots on his body that would make him moan and writhe and scream in ecstasy.

I opened a bedside drawer and pulled out a bottle of lube, slicking my cock to get it nice and wet. I was tempted to ease my way into him with maybe a finger or two, but the look of lust blazing in his eyes told me he wanted more than just my fingers.

Still, I wanted to make sure. "Would you like a finger first?" I asked.

"I don't need a finger, Daddy," he replied instantly. "I'm ready for you."

I smacked my lips together. I liked a confident bottom.

My cock ached at his words. I brought my swollen head to his pink hole and held it there, teasing it against his entrance. I could feel his hole twitching with anticipation against the tip of my dick.

When I finally entered him for the first time, his hips bucked against me wildly. I held back, giving him time to adjust to the length of my cock inside of him. As his body relaxed, he let out a low, deep moan from his chest and I knew he was ready.

If he was expecting me to take my time like I had exploring his body, he was in for a surprise. I let go of everything I'd been holding onto—the stress, the pain, the loneliness—and in that moment, all I could feel was the warmth of him encasing me. I unleashed.

I thrashed my hips into his body, slamming hard against him.

"Oh fuck yeah," he cried out, his fingers pinching into my skin, letting me feel his pleasure as our bodies moved as one.

"Fuck me, Daddy."

His eyes danced with an insatiability that spurred me on even further. I looked down at him, at my boy beneath me, and again I was struck by his transformation. Here he was, moaning and writhing under my sweaty body, giving me exactly what I wanted. Pleasing me like no other boy, no other man, had ever come close to pleasing me.

I increased the rhythm, thrusting into him harder and with even more force. The sight of him, the way he smelled, the way his body wrapped itself so perfectly around my cock...I let out a mighty roar and started coming.

The feel of my warm release pushed him over the edge. His groans met mine as he yelled out in pleasure. The force of our shared orgasm bound our bodies together, shaking, spasming, twisting, until finally...*finally*...the sensation began to subside.

I pulled up beside him, propping myself up on my elbow. I traced my finger along his jaw and up to his ear.

"So," he said, looking at me with contentment written all across his face. "You're sure I was worth the wait then?"

"Oh, my boy. I would have waited a lifetime for you."

I gently brushed my lips against his and he moaned ever so softly into our kiss.

"Will you hold me?" His voice was raw and tender. "I—I need your arms around me."

He was already beginning to drift off to sleep. My heart swelled at those words and I moved myself closer so that I could wrap him up in my arms and keep him there until morning. Although, really, that was nowhere near long enough.

If I had my way, I'd never let him out of my arms. His warm body pressed against mine just felt so right.

This.

Him.

Me.

Us.

I moved my head slightly so that my nose and chin gently rested against the nape of his neck. Any last, lingering doubts I may have had were banished from my mind.

I closed my eyes, wanting this moment to last forever. My eyelids grew heavier and heavier, and for the first time in three years, I fell into a blissfully deep, warm, uninterrupted sleep.

CHAPTER FIFTEEN

STIRLING

"Wait, wait, wait," Porter said, holding his hand up in mid-air. "How is that the guy who's the newest Daddy here is the only one of us with a boyfriend?"

I looked around at my three friends and shrugged.

"What can I say?" I said with a smile. "I took a DNA test and it turns out, I'm *that Daddy*."

The guys erupted with laughter and after a few moments, I joined in with them.

"Nice one," Hudson said, wiping away a tear from his face. "See, you start dating a younger guy and you're already picking up all the cool catchphrases."

It felt good to laugh and it felt good to be more open and able to talk to my friends like this. And throwing in a cool catchphrase every once in a while wasn't a bad thing either.

We were sitting in a large circular booth at The Laird. There was a jazz band playing and a few people milling around, but overall, the place was pretty quiet and chill.

Unlike my mind. Part of me still couldn't believe it. I had a boyfriend. As in an actual boyfriend who was a...boy.

"Well, I take full credit for it," Porter continued.

"Oh, do you now?" I said, unable to suppress my smirk. "And why would that be?"

"Isn't it obvious?" Porter said with an incredulous look splashed across his face. "My three-point plan? Remember? Duh."

Hudson rolled his eyes and groaned.

"Yeah, what he said," Steel said, tipping his head over in Hudson's direction.

"Hey, I did say it was guaranteed to work...and it worked. So, you're welcome my friend." And with that, Porter heartily slapped his hand across my back.

"Well actually, since you mentioned your three-point plan..." I began.

All three of them leaned in, huddled over the drinks, their eyes planted on me. God, I was a sucker for punishment.

"I need some advice. How do I take things...further?"

"How about you back it up a little and fill us in on exactly where you and Mikey are at?" Hudson, the voice of reason, suggested.

So I filled the guys in, skipping over some of the more private details of when Mikey had come over to my place the previous week and we'd made love for the first time. But I covered pretty much everything else, including the conversation we'd had about the kind of Daddy/boy dynamic we both wanted, and the thinking I'd been doing about what I wanted...sexually.

"I'm impressed, Stirling," Steel said once I was done. "It's amazing how much you've opened up to him. Very unlike you, but very good progress. And," he added, giving me a gentle elbow to the ribs, "your lips are doing that thing again."

I didn't even bother hiding my smile. I was happy and I didn't care who saw.

"So, it's sounding like you've got a pretty good idea of what you want, then," Hudson said.

"That's step one of my patented three-point plan," Porter chimed in.

"Oh, it's patented now, is it?" Steel said with a chuckle.

"Yep, just came through," Porter said, lifting his phone, and we all laughed.

"But how do I tell him?" I asked.

It was more of a plea really. I had to know. I was so desperate to break through whatever this invisible barrier was, I just didn't know how to.

"Is that true?" Steel asked. "You've figured out what you want?"

I nodded.

"Yeah. It is."

"Ooh," Porter practically squealed with excitement. "Do tell. What kind of kinky shit are you into, Stirling Bishop? I've been dying to know for years. We all have."

"Hey, speak for yourself," Steel said, his brows furrowing.

"Exactly," Hudson chimed in, shooting an annoyed look in Porter's direction. "You don't have to tell us anything you don't want to, Stirling, you know that."

"Thanks, I know that, Hudson. But it's not you guys I'm worried about telling. It's Mikey."

"What do you mean?" Porter asked.

"Mikey's opened up to me, so now I feel like I should... No wait, I don't feel like I *should*," I corrected myself. "I *want* to open up to him as well."

"That's a good sign," Steel said as he played with the rim of his glass. "It means you're comfortable enough to talk to him. That doesn't come easy for you, so if Mikey makes you feel like you want to talk, then that's a really good thing."

Hudson and Porter nodded in agreement.

"It is," I agreed. "This is the direction I feel I want to be moving in. I want to start talking, I want to begin living my life again, you know?"

I could see all three guys nodding their heads.

"You deserve it, Stirling. After everything you've been through, and are still going through, you deserve to be happy. You do get that, right?" Hudson asked, taking a sip of his drink, his eyes studying me carefully.

"I do," I said, nodding, rocking my whole torso with me. "This feels right, you guys. If anything, it feels years overdue."

"Which brings us to another very important point," Hudson said. "This is something Master X told me when I first joined Revolver."

"Master X?" I asked.

"He's the owner of Revolver," Steel answered. He looked over at Hudson with intense curiosity. "Wait, you've met Master X?"

Hudson shook his head.

"No, no one has. The man's identity is a complete mystery. But I did speak to him over the phone when I first joined."

"Ah, okay." Hudson's response seemed to satisfy Steel.

"The thing he taught me was this, Stirling. In the Daddy/boy relationship dynamic, there's a flipside to control, which is care."

"Care?" I asked, bringing the glass up to my lips.

"Yes, care," Hudson said. "Control is one side of the coin, care is the other. The care between the men in these Daddy/boy or Dom/sub relationships is just something on a whole new level, Stirling. It's not something that you see or hear as much about, but it's there. In fact, for me...care is the most important part."

"Not something you will ever see in C-grade porn," Steel teased with a playful smile.

"Who watches that? I've got a boyfriend, remember?" I joked, and the guys laughed.

When the guys settled down, Hudson continued talking. "There is something so beautiful and spiritual and primal that happens in the exchange of care between a Daddy and a boy that, well, until you experience it for yourself, Stirling, I don't think I can find the words to do it justice."

Hudson leaned back, the edges of his lips tugging at a smile, as the glimmer of a faded memory lit up his whole face.

I looked over at him. This giant beast of a man, this wall of muscle. Such a tough exterior that belied such a gentle, beautiful spirit. I was curious to know more about that side of him, but now wasn't the time for that.

"Wow."

It was all I could manage. I'd never realized there was more to it than just taking control. That part of it had never really sat right with me, but hearing about the flip side of control—care—struck a very deep chord within me.

I did have a caring, nurturing side and I felt something tugging within me, urging me to explore that side of myself more. I'd felt it already so many times with Mikey.

The time I'd seen him at Steel's party and had to place my feet on his back, I hadn't wanted to hurt him.

On our first date when he was nervous, not knowing where we were going, I had placed my hand on his leg to reassure him.

I'd picked him up and been there for him after he'd learned about his mom's diagnosis.

Looking after him.

Protecting him.

Caring for him.

It was all there within me. I'd been confused because all my life I thought that being a Daddy—and especially a Daddy who was into what I was into sexually—was solely about control. I'd literally only been seeing half of the story.

It was the care aspect that I was really drawn to. It felt like Fourth of July fireworks were going off inside of me. I was buzzing, elated at the discovery I'd made.

"Well, welcome to the Daddy club," Porter said, patting me on the back and lightening the mood instantly. "We're glad you finally joined us."

I rolled my eyes and smiled.

"Now tell me," he said, leaning in. "What kind of kinky shit are you into?"

"Porter!" Steel and Hudson cried out at the same time.

"What?! We're all friends here," Porter said, somewhat dejectedly. "Besides, we all know it's the quiet ones you gotta look out for."

"I think your bullshit has earned you the right to go get us a round of drinks," Hudson said, aiming his gaze squarely at Porter.

"Fair enough," Porter said, sliding himself out of the booth. "Same again?"

"Make mine a double," Hudson replied.

"Just a soda for me, thanks," I said.

Porter nodded and turned toward the bar.

"Don't talk about anything kinky while I'm gone. I don't want to miss anything," he yelled over his shoulder. I shook my head as I watched him walking away from us.

"He's one of a kind, that guy," I said.

"That he is," Steel agreed with a smirk. "But we love him."

"We do indeed."

"You don't have to tell us anything. We won't push you,"

Hudson said in that completely calm and non-judgemental way of his.

"Agreed," Steel added. "Based on what you've told us, Stirling, things are going well with you and Mikey. Maybe you should just relax and allow yourself to enjoy it a bit?"

It was good advice and it made sense. I should just relax and enjoy it. But I also felt that if I didn't talk honestly and openly with Mikey about what I wanted, I wouldn't be able to. So it was a catch-22 situation.

I mean, how do you tell someone that your fantasy involved you spanking them, then caressing them tenderly afterward?

I knew Mikey had said he wanted to serve, that it was all that he wanted to do, but he had also said *within reasonable limits*. What did that mean? Would a light spanking fit inside or outside of those limits? What if we weren't compatible, what would happen then?

"Your drinks, gentlemen," Porter said, returning to the table and saving me from the torrent of unanswered questions running through my head. As he passed Hudson his drink, he added, "And a double for you."

"Thanks," Hudson replied.

"Did I miss anything?" Porter asked, rubbing his hands together.

"No, we just told Stirling—again—that he doesn't have to tell us anything," Hudson said, a little pointedly.

"If you don't want to tell us anything, my friend," Porter said looking at me, "then you absolutely don't have to. You know me, I was just kidding around. I don't want to make you uncomfortable. But we are here for you and we do have some experience in this area, whether it's relationship stuff or Daddy/boy stuff. All I'm saying is, we're here for you. Talk to us...or not. It's totally up to you."

I took a mouthful of soda, swishing it around in my mouth before swallowing it down.

"I know. Thanks, guys, I appreciate you being here for me," I said. And I meant it. But I also knew I had to figure this one out on my own.

The thing that struck me the most about what Mikey had said when he'd told me what he was into was how he had felt like something was missing for him.

In a way, I felt exactly the same. As embarrassing as it was to admit, ever since I first saw it in a grainy C-grade porno as a teenager, I'd felt an instant attraction to spanking. But in the many years since my first time watching that scene, and browsing countless websites and online forums, I'd never come across anything that felt like what I wanted.

Because for me, it wasn't something that was humiliating or degrading, or something that made the boy feel powerless or used. It was something that was sacred. Something shared between two people, an exchange of energy between them that drew them closer and connected them in a special way.

And yes, the visuals of it turned me on too. The skin-on-skin sound of the slapping, the feel of the friction it generated, and the pattern it left on a guy's ass, fuck...*that* drove me wild. Or at least, it drove my imagination wild.

I had never done anything spanking related before, not even a mild slap on the ass during sex with Richard. Despite that, I felt the attraction of it pull me in more than ever before.

I could feel the thickness of my erection pressing against my jeans. I looked around, worried, as if my friends could somehow tell what was happening in my pants. They couldn't, of course, but I needed to change the topic. Fast.

"So, Steel," I said. "What's the deal with you and Mikey's friend, Nick?"

Porter winked at me.

"Yeah, Steel," he added playfully. "The guy was practically eye fucking you all night on the yacht."

"Give me a break, you guys," Steel said as his cheeks and neck flushed a bright red.

"And I couldn't help but notice," Hudson joined in, "that there was a good ten, maybe fifteen minutes at my party when both you and Nick mysteriously disappeared."

"Oh was there now?" I said, turning to face Steel, unable to wipe the grin off my face. "Do tell, Mr. Crawford. Do tell."

"Oh *now* you all want to get the juicy details," Porter exclaimed, throwing his hands up in the air.

"There are no juicy details," Steel said, looking down, uncharacteristically subdued. "Nothing happened."

The dejection in his voice made us all believe him and we stopped kidding around.

"Do you want to talk about it?" Hudson asked, a look of concern written all over his face.

"Nope," Steel said, and with that he brought his drink to his lips and took a big gulp, swinging his head back and slamming the empty glass back down on the table.

The three of us looked at each other, unsure of what to say next. As usual, Porter was happy to jump in and fill the silence, regaling us all with his wild—and of course, kinky—adventures at Revolver the previous weekend.

I looked over at Steel and made a mental note to talk to him about this more, when it was just him and me, one on one.

I let out a yawn as I looked at the time on my phone. It was just a few minutes past ten, but the stress and anxiety of the court case from the past few days was catching up with me. Thankfully, no one noticed, absorbed in the intimate details of Porter's story.

My thoughts returned to Mikey. Yes, things were moving

fast. We were getting to know each other more quickly, and on a much deeper level, than I had expected.

He had stepped up. He had worked through his trust issues and taken a massive chance in opening himself up to me. Now, it was my turn.

Could I do it? Could I step up and tell Mikey what I wanted from him?

From...us?

CHAPTER SIXTEEN

MIKEY

The last week had been a crazy rollercoaster ride.

Finding out about my mom's diagnosis was awful. Beyond awful. I was truly terrified of losing her. I'd never been so scared in my whole life.

Nick and Ben were both working that night, so I'd turned to Stirling. I went from the lowest of lows to the highest of highs, learning about the diagnosis, then making love—*and becoming boyfriends*—with Stirling, all in one night.

The way Stirling came through for me that night showed me I could trust him. Yes, maybe I was moving fast by "normal" people's standards, but who wants to be normal? For me, it was progress. I'd resisted jumping in head first straight away, as much as I wanted to. I'd asked questions and cleared things up right from the start, even though it was awkward and it would have been easier not to.

Now I'd earned the right to relax a little and just go with it.

The man was the Daddy of my dreams—and I wanted to enjoy it.

He understood me, all of me, in a way no other man ever had. Stirling was erasing the last remaining memories I had of Brian and it felt so freeing. He treated me so well. He was strong, kind, genuinely thoughtful, and so understanding.

His massive cock plunging into me didn't hurt either, at least not in the bad way. It hurt in the *very* good way.

How that man had survived twelve whole months with no release was still something I couldn't quite wrap my brain around. How no other boy had jumped on him and claimed him as their own was an equally perplexing mystery. But what did I care? It meant that he was mine. All mine.

The end of the drought had released an insatiable appetite in him, one that he needed to be fulfilled every night, at least once, if not more. Not that you'd ever hear me complaining about it. I was more than ready, willing, and able to please...my *Daddy*.

I never thought anyone would truly understand me, and my desire to serve and please. I just assumed that I would have to settle for someone who kinda, sorta got it...but didn't fully get it on a deeper level. Like when someone just nods their heads as if they get what you're saying, but you can see in their eyes that they don't really get it.

Or worse. I'd meet yet another guy who would distort my willingness to please and to serve, twisting it into something it wasn't. Something dirty. Shameful. Bad. Those words—*and worse*—wounded me as much as being with Stirling was healing me.

Stirling got it straight away. Like, he *really* got it. And he never judged me for it, never made me feel like there was anything wrong with me for wanting what I wanted.

I did wish he would talk a little more. I could tell a part of him was still holding back. As great as it was that he understood me, I wanted to know him better so I could give him everything he wanted too.

But I knew that would all come...in normal people time.

"Hey, loverboy, snap out of it," Nick said, clicking his fingers in my face. "You're meant to be helping."

"I am helping," I lied as I looked over at Nick.

It was mid-morning and we were in the backstage area of The Tank Top, the go-go bar where Nick danced. The whole place was dimly lit and had the dry muskiness of a locker room, but with more glitter and way more pink everywhere.

The club was closed, but Nick wanted to try on a few different looks, so of course, he brought me along to help. I loved spending time with him, and besides, it had been a while since we'd caught up in person. I was a little...busy with my Daddy.

He was standing in front of a full-length mirror, one of the old-school Hollywood ones that had light bulbs all around it. His hair was in a messy bun on the top of his head, and he was adjusting himself, shifting from foot to foot, inspecting himself in the mirror. He was holding his shirt halfway up, revealing his big, soft, hairy belly.

"Now, do these jeans make my ass look big?" he asked, not turning away from his reflection.

"You know they do," I replied, then I added for good measure, "and you know you want them to."

Countless hours at the gym spent doing squats were paying off. The guy was borderline obsessed about making his thick booty even thicker.

"Good, because I really want it to..."

"Pop?" I suggested with a playful smile. "Why are you wearing jeans onstage, though? Don't you normally wear...less?"

"Ah, see this is where being a magician comes in handy." Nick turned so that he was looking away from me. He reached his hands around and cupped his ass. As he looked over his shoulder at me, he said, "Now you see them...and now you don't."

And with that, he pulled the denim covering his ass cheeks apart, revealing the jeans to be a pair of assless chaps that showed off his thick, meaty behind.

"Got it," I said as Nick gave his ass a wiggle, getting a nice bounce out of each cheek. He kinda made me wish my booty was a little thicker too. Mine was like a pancake compared to his. Before I could voice my slight jealousy, we heard a loud thud from outside the dressing room.

"Is anyone else here?" I asked.

"Shouldn't be," Nick said, walking to the front of the bar, his ass still exposed. I followed close behind. Over his shoulder he asked me, "You did lock up when we came in, right?"

Shit, did I?

"I, uh..."

We stepped out into the dim, empty bar section and saw a man's figure walking, or rather stumbling, toward us.

"I'm sorry sir...we're not actually open yet," Nick called out. "Doors open at five if you'd like to come back then."

"Shut up, fatty." The stumbling man's voice echoed through the empty place and I froze.

That voice made my stomach drop to the floor. I thought I was going to be sick. The man stumbling toward us, getting closer and closer...was Brian.

I didn't know what to do. I was paralyzed with fear. I may have left the front door unlocked, but how did he know where we were? And what did he want from me?

Nick and I stood at one end of the bar, Brian at the other. Nick stood in front of me, protectively, shielding me from the dark outline at the other end of the bar.

"You need to go, Brian, or I'm calling the police," Nick said in his forceful *don't-fuck-with-me* voice.

"Didn't I tell you to shut the fuck up, fatty?"

He was slurring his words. He'd been drinking, I could tell. I'd heard that same drunken slur before, way too many times. But it was eleven in the morning on a Wednesday and he was already at least half drunk. That was a new low, even for him.

"If you don't leave right now, Brian, I'm calling the police," Nick said, moving slowly toward him. He had his phone in his hands and waved it at Brian. "I'm serious. Leave. Right now."

"Fine," Brian said.

As he tried to move, he knocked over a bar stool, which crashed loudly onto the floor. He tried to walk closer to us, to me, but Nick stepped in his way and blocked him. I was glued to the end of the bar, my fingers gripping it so tightly my knuckles were white.

"You think you're so good, don't you?" he spat the words out. His bloodshot eyes met mine. "Think you can just ignore me when I text you, huh?"

I was shaking, my body was locked in a fear that wouldn't let me move, wouldn't let me speak. I just wanted him gone. I knew Nick was there and would never let anything happen to me, but I just wanted Brian gone. Out of the bar. Out of my life. I didn't want to have anything more to do with him.

Why was he continuing to torture me like this?

"Well I've got some news for you, Mikey boy. Sweet, innocent, little Mikey boy. Or at least that's what you'd like everyone to think, isn't it?"

"Brian," Nick puffed his chest out, blocking Brian. "Get out now."

There was silence, bone-gripping silence. I was praying he wouldn't do anything stupid or violent. I just wanted him to go. Why wasn't he going?

After what felt like an eternity, he turned around and left. I looked past Nick and saw him making his way to the door, still unsteady on his feet. I walked up to Nick and placed my hand on his shoulder. My protector, as always.

We both watched Brian leave. As he got to the door, he turned around and yelled, "But no one will think you're innocent when I show the world the video you made for me. Remember the one I'm talking about, Mikey? Of course you do, you little slut."

And with that, he stumbled out through the door. Nick ran over and locked it, before running back to me. Tears were streaming down my face as Nick pressed me into his body, his heavy arms securing me tightly.

"It's okay, it's okay, Mikey," he said as he stroked my hair.

But it wasn't okay. Nothing was okay. Brian was cruel and mean and hellbent on destroying my life. And with that video, he would be able to do just that.

Nick let go of me and pulled out a stool for me to sit on. The sight of him walking around to the other side of the bar to get some water made me smile for a moment.

"You're still wearing your assless chaps," I said with a faint giggle.

"It's my superhero costume," he said as he slid the glass of water across the bar.

I gulped it down. I hadn't realized that being a shitscared loser could be such thirsty work. Now I did.

"Has he got a video of you, Mikey?" Nick asked, concern written all over his face.

I nodded, fighting back the tears that wanted to fall again, but I was determined not to let them. Even though it had only been a one-time thing, and even though he had sworn he would delete it, I was pretty sure he had lied and kept it. I had even suspected it at the time, but as usual, I'd just let it slide, not wanting to say or do anything to set him off. I had kind of just hoped he'd forgotten about it. As if I would be that lucky.

"How...how revealing is it?"

I looked up and Nick's brown eyes were chock full of worry.

Right at that moment, my phone vibrated. It was a text message. From Brian. It was the video. Fuck, he really did have it.

Another text.

Brian: *The whole world will see who you really are, Mikey.*

The tears fell down my face as I slid the phone across to Nick. He just read the text, leaving the video alone.

"Shit," he said with a dispirited sigh. "Well, you know what you have to do, Mikey."

I looked up at him, confused. I didn't. I had no freaking idea what to do. What could I do? I had zero options. Brian was going to release the video and my life would be over.

"Wh-what?" I wheezed in between wiping the tears off my face.

"You have to tell Stirling," he said.

Oh fuck. Stirling. Hearing his name made it even worse. I let out a loud sob. There was no way he would stay with me. Not now. Not once he saw the video with his own eyes. That would be it.

Because of one stupid decision I'd made in the past, Brian would be able to ruin my future with Stirling.

"Are you crazy, Nick?" I said. "I can't, I can't tell Stirling about this."

"Uh, yeah you can, and yeah you will, Mikey," Nick said forcefully, as he cocked his head to the side, giving me a toned-down version of his *don't-fuck-with-me* look from before.

"I can't," I said.

"Why?"

Nick put his hand on his hip and stared at me with a

ferociousness I hadn't seen in him since he'd stood up to those bullies back in high school.

"Because..." The tears started up again. "Because he'll leave me, Nick."

Nick came around and gave me another hug.

"He won't leave you, Mikey," he said as I sobbed into his chest. "Not if he's the man you think he is. But you have to tell him. It's the only thing you can do here."

Nick's words echoed in my head. I felt trapped. I *was* trapped, backed into a corner with no good options. Brian was going to release the video for everyone to see. And I was going to lose my boyfriend. They were the only two guaranteed outcomes here.

No wait, there was one more.

At the age of twenty-four, I had proven beyond a shadow of a doubt that I was still a coward, someone so pathetic and helpless that he couldn't even stand up for himself and needed to hide behind his best friend.

A coward whose life was about to be over.

CHAPTER SEVENTEEN

STIRLING

I knew I had to do it.

As I stared at Mikey's front door, with takeout in one hand and about to knock on the door with the other, all I could think about was telling him. Finally telling him.

As much as I would never admit it to him, Porter's three-point plan did have some merit. I knew what I wanted—step one. And if I wanted to get it—step three—I would have to do the one thing that I sucked the most at. That pesky step two—talk.

Mikey deserved it too. I saw the courage it had taken him to open up to me, and it made me want him even more. I wanted Mikey to know me, to know all of me.

Mikey always talked about how he liked the strong, silent type. That was all well and good, but being silent wasn't what made a man strong. Sometimes, even a quiet guy had to find a way to speak up, to share, to expose himself and be vulnerable. Because that right there takes real strength.

I knocked on the door and from the moment Mikey opened it, I knew something was wrong with him. He did seem genuinely happy to see me, but he felt a little...off. A little flat. Like there was something wrong, something he wasn't telling me. My stomach clenched at the thought that anything bad had happened to him.

He busied himself setting the table, but he wasn't his usual chatty self. How the hell was I going to find out what was wrong with him then? Oh, that's right, that whole pesky talking thing.

I followed him into the kitchen and watched as he opened up the containers of food and grabbed plates and cutlery.

"How's work going?" I asked.

"Yeah, good," he responded unenthusiastically, avoiding eye contact.

"How's Nick? Any crazy adventures to report?"

I hoped that might maybe earn me a smile at least. But no, just an offhand comment about *Nick being Nick*, and that was it.

As we sat down at the table, it hit me. I mentally slapped myself for being so stupid and missing it. Mikey was looking at his food but not eating it, just moving it around the plate with his fork.

"Mikey," I began, somewhat apprehensively. "How's your mom doing?"

He looked up at me, *finally*, his blue eyes cold and torn like shards of glass.

"She's doing okay," he said, and for the briefest of moments, his face softened a little. He gave me a look that I couldn't read before returning to pushing food around his plate.

"Mikey, can you look at me please?"

Something was definitely wrong and I needed to find out what. It didn't seem to be work, or Nick, or his mom, so I was all out of ideas. I needed him to tell me. But first, I needed him to look at me, which, for some strange reason, he was stubbornly refusing to do.

I looked at him for a moment, silently willing him to lift his head up to look at me. Nothing. I was fighting the growing irritation inside of me, more out of not knowing what was going on than anything directed at him. I was becoming frustrated. How could I help him when I didn't even know what the issue was?

"Mikey?" I asked, trying to keep my tone gentle but firm at the same time.

Without saying anything, he got up abruptly from the table and walked to the living room. What the hell was going on with him?

I got up and followed him. I placed my hand on his shoulder, to slow him down and to have him turn and look at me. As he turned, and as his eyes met mine, I could see they were filled with tears.

"Mikey, what's wrong? Please tell me. I want to help you."

"You can't," he said, his voice flat and cold as he pulled away from me and sat down on one end of the couch.

I sat down at the other end, giving him plenty of space, and said, "I can help you, but only if you tell me what's going on."

"What's going on," he snapped. His whole body jolted upright. "You want to know what's going on? Really, Stirling?"

I was taken aback by his tone, surprised at how ferocious it was, but I nodded my head.

"Hell yeah," I said, trying to keep my demeanor steady. "Tell me, Mikey. Tell me what's going on, what's gotten you this upset."

And just like that, the fire that raged within him subsided and he was back to being the soft, gentle Mikey that I knew. Whatever that flare-up was, wherever it had come from, it disappeared just as quickly.

He rolled himself up into a little ball at the end of the couch, tucking his legs into his body, and hugging his knees tightly.

He looked up at me through his long lashes and murmured so softly I had to strain to hear it, "You're going to leave me when you find out."

My breath caught in my throat. That was a curveball I hadn't seen coming. Had he done something bad, something that would make me want to leave him? Oh god, had he...cheated on me?

"Tell me, Mikey," I said tensely.

Part of me wanted to add something reassuring, something about me not leaving him no matter what it was, but I couldn't lie to him. If he was about to tell me that he had cheated on me, I didn't think I could take it. Not again. Once was painful enough.

A long silence fell between us.

"My ex, Brian, came to see me yesterday morning. I was helping Nick set up at The Tank Top when he barged in. He was drunk."

"He was drunk in the morning?" I asked.

Mikey let out a sigh. A tired, exasperated one.

"Yeah," he said as he looked around the living room, his eyes desperate to focus on anything other than me.

I sat up straighter.

"Did he hurt you?"

I studied his face and body for any signs of bruises.

Mikey shook his head. "Physically, no."

"But...he did something?"

Mikey's face froze. The only movement was his Adam's apple bobbing up and down, almost violently, in his throat.

"When we were together," he said into his chest, "I made a video for him."

He looked up at me and it took my brain a few seconds to connect the dots.

"Oh," I managed to say.

Mikey blushed and looked down again.

"It was a...private video. Just for him. No one else was ever meant to see it. But now..." his voice trailed off.

"But now what, Mikey?"

I could see him starting to tremble, but I needed him to tell me. I needed to know what I was dealing with here.

"But now he's threatened to release the video for everyone to see."

"Oh, Mikey," I said. "My poor boy. Come here."

He looked up at me, his eyes wide open. The hurt, pain, and shame were written across his face.

I released a breath I hadn't realized I was holding as I motioned for him to come over to me. He needed the safety of my touch and I wanted to give it to him so badly. I was going to take care of him and look after my boy. I'd figure out the details later but for now, all I needed was to reassure him, and the best way to do that was to hold him close to me.

"No," he said softly. "I don't want to."

His words tore at my heart, twisting it a hundred different ways.

"Mikey," I said. "I'm not going to leave you because of this."

"You haven't seen the video yet."

The sting of hurt in his words was unmissable. My protective instinct kicked in and flooded my chest with anger at what that asshole was doing to my boy, and the overwhelming need to just look after Mikey and protect him from all of this.

"I don't need to see the video, Mikey," I said as I slowly, deliberately shuffled down the couch to be nearer to him. I wanted to be closer, but I didn't want to surprise him, or make him uncomfortable, in any way.

I reached out, and before my hand could touch his, he lunged into me, slamming his body into mine, hugging me closer and tighter than he'd ever held me before. His body was shaking and I could feel the wet, warm tears sinking into my shirt. I wrapped my arms around him and stroked his hair, giving him all the time he needed.

Even though he was crying and scared and shaking, this felt so right. Having him near me, telling me what had happened, stepping up to help him, it all felt like it was meant to be.

When he had calmed down, I placed my hands on his shoulders and pulled him back.

I looked straight into his wide, blue eyes and said, "Mikey Harrison, you are one of the strongest people I know. What you did for your last Daddy, when you were with him, was special. Nothing can change that. And what he is doing now is wrong. But he's the one who's doing the wrong thing. Not you. You haven't done anything wrong."

Mikey blinked hard, as if he were having a hard time believing what I was saying.

"Really? You mean that?" he asked in a voice so sweet and tender that it almost made me cry.

"I do," I said as I brushed a loose strand of hair from his forehead. "You wanted to please your Daddy. That's a beautiful, sacred thing, Mikey. Unfortunately, your previous Daddy didn't deserve it. And now, he's abusing the trust you put in him. He is not a good man."

"He's the wrong type of Daddy," Mikey said.

"That's right, my beautiful boy," I said, and my chest lightened a little as I could see Mikey beginning to relax, beginning to trust me, beginning to believe that I wasn't going to leave him.

"And one more thing," I said.

"What?" Mikey asked, and I could hear the worry creeping back into his voice.

"Thank you," I said as I gently kissed his forehead.

"Why—why are you thanking me?" he asked, scrunching up his nose in that cute way of his.

"Because you told me, Mikey. I know it couldn't have been easy for you. I get that, and that's why I appreciate it so much."

"I was so scared," he began. "I really thought you would leave me."

His lower lip started to tremble, but I could also see the steely determination within him, fighting back the tears. He really was strong, so much stronger than he realized.

"We're going to deal with this together, okay?" I said as I took his soft fingers in my hand.

He nodded.

"Yep," he said.

"And Mikey," I said, squeezing his hand firmly. "I want you to promise me that you will always talk to me. You will always come to me and tell me if you ever have any problem, or anything at all, going on in your life, okay?"

"Okay," he said with a quiet sincerity.

"You promise?" I asked.

"Yes, I promise." And with that, he fell back into my arms, his warm body pressed against mine, molded so perfectly like it had always belonged there.

I smiled, relieved. He'd had me worried for a moment. I had no idea what he was going to say, and the thought of it being something bad, something truly bad, had petrified me. I was falling deeper and deeper for Mikey. The thought of losing him filled me with such an aching sadness that I didn't ever want to think about that again.

I pressed him in closer as I felt the familiar tightness return to my throat. Mikey was strong and he was brave. He'd told me something he was clearly uncomfortable with and ashamed about. He honestly thought I would leave him, but he had found the courage to tell me anyway.

Not like me.

Even though I knew this wasn't the right time, I couldn't keep delaying it for much longer. I would have to step up and finally tell Mikey everything.

I had to become the Daddy my boy needed me to be.

I wanted to become the Daddy I knew I had in me.

CHAPTER EIGHTEEN

MIKEY

Over the next two weeks, the rollercoaster ride that was my life only continued.

Telling Stirling about Brian's threat to mess up my life by releasing the video was all sorts of scary. I was hands-down sure he would leave me. And I wouldn't have blamed him either.

It was a lot to deal with. With the way the internet works, everyone would have ended up seeing that video sooner or later if Brian had posted it online. These things spread like wildfire, and once something goes online, you can never undo it.

Everyone would have seen it—Stirling's friends, his employees—why would the guy stick around after that?

But I hadn't been giving him enough credit. Not only did Stirling not leave me like I thought he would, he stepped up in the most incredible way. Well, him and his three friends. The unofficial Daddy counsel of Daylesford.

Steel sent Brian a cease and desist letter, reminding him that

Dayelsford had some of the strongest revenge porn laws in the country and warning him that any distribution of the video would result in a lawsuit.

Porter did some digging. Bars in Daylesford needed at least eight different types of licenses and permits. Brian may have been an asshole but he was a pedantic asshole. It took Porter a while but he was able to uncover that Brian's bar didn't have the correct licence to play background music.

So he did what any responsible mayor's chief of staff would do. He authorized an audit to be undertaken, with an inspector sent out to ensure, as he put it, "that public safety was maintained." Because, you know, if those royalties didn't get paid...

Hudson, the sweet, gentle giant that he was, revoked Brian's gym membership. He only ever really went to the gym to check out younger guys anyway, so I knew that one would hurt him.

And all four men vowed to never set foot in The Laird ever again. That really meant a lot, because it was their favorite bar and had been for so many years.

When they all came over for dinner one night, Porter said, "We couldn't decide whether the guy was more of a dick or an ass. So we decided he's a dickass. And there's no way in hell we can go to a bar owned by a dickass."

"Daddies will always support other Daddies," Steel added. "But when they do shit like this, we don't stand for it."

Their support was beyond anything I could have expected, and I appreciated it so much. But there was one man who kept surprising me more and more each day.

My boyfriend.

My Daddy.

Stirling.

Throughout all of this, he didn't flinch. Not even for a

second. His support meant the world to me, and in a funny way, this whole ordeal with Brian actually brought us closer.

I was walking back home after finishing a gig downtown. Nick and some of the other guys were hitting up a few bars. They'd asked if I wanted to join them, but I'd told Ma I'd take her to the doctor's the following morning, so I took a raincheck. I wanted to have an early night and be fresh for the morning.

Even though it helped a lot having Stirling in my life while everything was going on with my mom, her situation was still very scary and unknown.

The upcoming doctor's visit was going to focus on looking at some drug treatments that she might want to consider, in order to try and delay the deterioration of her condition for as long as possible. She was starting to become more forgetful and she had lost her balance twice in the last week.

The thought of her condition getting worse made me so sick it hurt, but I had to be strong for her. And having Stirling in my life, being strong for me, made it that much easier.

It was still relatively early in the evening and there were quite a few people walking around on the streets. I was happy to wander slowly, taking my time and doing a little window shopping. I saw a cute pair of striped navy and white shorts that I knew would make my booty pop, and Stirling's eyes too. I chuckled to myself as I realized that *booty pop* had somehow made its way into my vernacular.

I'd been working a lot, and earning crazy good tips, so my savings were looking better than ever. I had been saving up to cover the cost of my studies but they were, at this point at least, slightly delayed.

I had taken Ma's advice and decided to take the entrance test exam again. There was no harm in trying. Maybe she was right, maybe the timing just wasn't right the first time or something. I wasn't entirely convinced but I didn't have anything to lose, so why not at least give it another go and know for sure? The next slot for the entrance exam was still a few weeks off, though, which meant I could afford those super cute shorts.

There was a light breeze in the air as the temperature started to drop. I zipped my hoodie up as I reached the front window of Montrachet, the fanciest French restaurant in Daylesford. The dimly lit interior looked warm and inviting.

This would be the perfect place for a romantic dinner with Stirling. I knew he was more of a burger and fries guy than a coq au vin guy, but still, I wanted to see the way his body filled out a suit, accentuating his broad, built-up shoulders, making him look so masculine, so full. Just the thought of it was enough to stir my cock to life.

Maybe he could even fuck me wearing the suit? Now that would be hot. Very hot. Stirling dressed up looking all sorts of masculine and powerful, fucking me from behind. His face doing that thing, that kinda hot, kinda weird-looking contortion thing where his lips stretched wide and his eyes looked like they were about to pop out of his head. His green eyes sparkling with lust and desire for me.

The exact same green eyes I was looking at right now, having dinner at a small table near the back of the restaurant.

A small table...for two.

I blinked hard a few times, convinced I was seeing things. It couldn't be Stirling. He'd told me he'd be spending the evening at home, fixing the leaky showerhead he'd been putting off.

What I was looking at didn't make any sense.

But unless he had a secret twin brother, that was definitely him, sitting there having dinner. The man he was with looked to be about the same age as Stirling, maybe a few years older given his receding hairline and thin, wiry frame. He was well dressed though, a little too well dressed to be having dinner at one of the nicest restaurants in town with *my* boyfriend.

My stomach twisted as I looked at the two men, staring at them with such a fierce intensity it was a wonder the window didn't crack. They obviously couldn't see me, but Stirling was looking at the man intently.

He seemed different. He looked different. His fingers were interlaced on the table. He was sitting more upright than usual and he was more dressed up than I'd ever seen him. The dark gray blazer he was wearing brought out the olive complexion in his face and made him look handsome in a way I couldn't connect with.

I wanted to see him dressed up and in a suit, but sitting across the table from me at a romantic restaurant, not across from...whoever the fuck this guy was. I looked around, trying to figure out what to do. The bad feeling in my stomach crawled up into my chest and settled in my throat.

Just relax.

I took a breath, trying to calm myself down. I was sure there had to be a rational explanation for what I was seeing.

Until the man leaned in closer. I moved in closer too, my nose pressing against the window. I didn't care if I looked like a crazy stalker standing outside a restaurant, all I cared about was what was going on there.

The man slid his hand along the table and grabbed Stirling's hand. Stirling flinched and sharply pulled his hand away from the man. My heart was thumping in my chest, my mouth dry and slightly open.

The man didn't relent, he kept leaning in closer and closer toward Stirling. He reached his hand around the back of Stirling's neck. I started to feel faint, short breaths caught in my chest. I couldn't believe what was happening.

And then, in one foul swoop, the man leaned in for a...kiss?

I couldn't look, I had to turn away. I fell back from the window and stumbled the first few steps away from the restaurant, my hand covering my mouth. What the fuck had I just seen?

Oh god, oh god, oh god...

Everything started spinning, but all I knew was that I had to keep walking. I had to keep moving and put as much space between me and that restaurant as I could. The white-hot heat of tears pricked my eyes and, seconds later, started cascading down my face. The tightness in my chest made it hard to breath, but I kept moving.

How could Stirling have done this to me?

I quickened my pace, realizing I was still about five blocks away from my apartment. All I wanted to do was get home, shut the door, and scream. I started walking faster, the cool night air hitting my flushed face with a burning sting.

I broke out into a jog, then I ran. It was like the running version of ugly crying, arms flailing about and tears cascading down my cheeks, my whole face red and puffy. But I didn't care. My mind was racing as fast as my feet were carrying me. I just needed to get home, back to where it was safe and I could curl myself up into a ball and hide away from the world.

After everything I'd told him, after everything we'd shared, after how *good* it was between us, how could he do this? I was so confused, and angry at him, but I was more furious with myself.

How could I let myself be hurt, betrayed, and lied to by a man?

Again!

I reached my apartment out of breath and panting wildly, but relieved to be home. I fumbled with the keys, my hands trembling, and let myself in. I yelled out for Ben, but he wasn't home. That's right, he was working the nightshift.

I kicked off my shoes and dropped my bag on the floor as I raced into my bedroom, slamming the door shut behind me. I dove into my bed and pulled the covers up, wrapping them around me tightly.

I closed my eyes. But the image of Stirling at the restaurant was burned into my memory, scalding my mind like a hot cup of coffee. I flinched, tossing under the covers, desperate to erase it from my mind, but even with my eyes shut, it was all I could see.

I started sobbing. Loud, violent cries escaped me. My whole body rocked. It just wasn't fair. All I wanted was to find someone who would love me, protect me, look after me. Fuck, at this point I'd take someone who just didn't lie to me and treat me like a piece of garbage.

I'd thought Stirling was that guy. I'd thought he was different from the others. That he'd be the one to understand me, the one to look after and love me.

But how well did I really know him? I knew he hadn't told me everything, he was still holding something back from me. Probably a lot of things.

Maybe he'd been dating younger guys all his life and just used the whole *I've never been with a younger guy* routine to lure me in.

Or maybe he was married and he was having dinner with his...husband.

Or maybe, he wasn't into younger guys anymore...because of me.

My mind was spiraling out of control. I lay on my bed sobbing, my whole life turned upside down, the neverending rollercoastering taking yet another turn.

I pulled my pillow out from under my head. I needed to get it out of me, this bloodcurdling rage that was starting to boil in my veins. All the pent up anger caused by guys who thought that they could just walk all over me and do whatever, say whatever, and that I would just put up with it. The fury and the embarrassment battled for dominance in my chest.

I was done with being a victim.

I was done taking shit from anyone.

I was done with Stirling.

I grabbed the pillow and pulled it over my face. With everything I had in me, I let out the loudest, angriest scream of my life.

CHAPTER NINETEEN

STIRLING

I shouldn't have done it.

Sitting across the table from him, listening to him drone on and on—about himself, of course—the regret was building up inside of me with every self-centered, egotistical word that he spoke.

But it had surprised me, so out of the blue, a text from Richard that he was back in town. He wanted to catch up, see how I was doing. Ha, that was rich coming from the guy who not only broke my heart by cheating on me, but also helped himself to half of everything I had.

I shouldn't have replied. I had my evening nicely planned. A quick fix-it job on the leaking showerhead I should have looked at weeks ago, followed by some takeout and a movie on the couch. Nice, simple, relaxing.

Mikey was at work, otherwise we would have spent the evening together. When he wasn't working, we spent pretty much every night together, alternating between my place and his.

I'd gotten to meet his brother, this time with my ass inside of my pants, and spend some time with him. I liked Ben, he was a nice guy, and I liked Mikey's apartment, but I liked having him at my place more. There was no one else around, which gave us all the privacy we needed.

I really shouldn't have accepted Richard's dinner invitation.

He clicked his fingers at the server, obnoxiously waving his arm in the air until the man walked over.

"Sir," the server spoke calmly, showing more restraint than I would have.

"I'll have another double vodka," Richard said, then looked over at me. "What about you, babe?"

I bristled under the heaviness of my jacket, my fists clenched under the table. He had known I hated being called babe when we were dating, but he'd probably forgotten that. He had a talent for forgetting things he didn't want to remember.

"I'm fine, thanks," I muttered, and the server left.

We were only up to entrées, but at this rate I didn't think I'd make it to the mains. Why did he even bring me to this place? He must have forgotten I hated places like this. I looked around. It was a nice restaurant, but way too fancy, way too pretentious, so in other words, Richard's perfect place.

I had to pull out a navy jacket from the back of my wardrobe just so that I could at least look semi-decent. It had been a few years since I'd worn it and it must have shrunk in my wardrobe or something. It was pressing in uncomfortably around my shoulders and I had to unfasten the buttons as soon as we were seated, for fear of them popping off by themselves.

"Why did you want to see me?" I asked him. But really, I was asking myself that question. Why did I say yes to meeting

Richard? I could have just said no or even ignored his text completely. I didn't owe the guy anything.

So why do it? Why did I agree to meet this obnoxious, overdressed, arrogant man who chewed his pan-fried scallops with his mouth open and called me babe?

The honest answer was, I didn't really know. I wasn't angry at the guy anymore. What had happened was in the past, the distant past. I had literally zero feelings left for him. In fact, I was on the minus scale when it came to even thinking about Richard.

I guess some small part of me was curious in a way. I mean, we had spent seven years together. It was my longest relationship. There had been a time when this man knew me better than anyone else in the world.

But that period of my life was over, well and truly. Sitting across from him, it struck me that he had never really known me. And that part wasn't actually his fault. It was mine. The reason Richard never got to know me was because I never opened up to him. Not really.

Not in the way I wanted to open up to Mikey. The thought of Mikey made me smile, and I wanted nothing more than to get out of this place, out of this ill-fitting jacket, and feel his warm body pressed into mine as we sat on my sofa watching a movie.

"I thought it'd be good to catch up," Richard said.

His insincerity snapped me out of my Mikey daydream and my smile vanished at the sight of the half-chewed scallop in his mouth. Why did the guy not close his mouth when he ate like any normal person?

"Besides, I heard the court case is coming to an end," he said as he put down his knife and fork. He'd finally finished chewing, thank fuck. "Which means, payday."

He rubbed his hands in glee and I scoffed. Of course,

wherever there was money involved, there was Richard sniffing around like the greedy, unscrupulous vulture that he was.

"Wait, how do you even know what's going on with the case?" I asked, and he must have picked up on the irritation in my voice, or on my face, or in my hands that I now had balled up on the table in fists, my knuckles white with seething rage.

"Whoa, relax, babe," he said, pausing while the server returned with his drink.

"Thank you," I said to the server, because like so many other things, good manners weren't particularly high on Richard's priority list.

"I was working on a story a month or two ago about the parent company of the retirement village your folks were at. They were involved in a whole bunch of shady financial shit." He hesitated, looking at me expectantly. "So I take it you didn't read it then?" I shook my head.

"No, I must have missed it," I said.

"Well that's too bad, because if you had bothered to read it, you might have been interested to know that a lot of the non-disclosure agreements the staff had signed expired recently."

I stared at him blankly.

"Which means," he continued with a self-satisfied smirk, "that witnesses who might have previously been barred from testifying, might now be more...forthcoming."

I shuffled in my seat. It pained me to give him any credit at all, but on this one thing and one thing only, he was actually being useful. Not that I was going to tell him that.

"I'll let Steel know, thanks," I muttered.

"Don't mention it, babe," he said, taking a large sip of his drink.

When he looked at me again, he was different, softer. Maybe the buzz of the three drinks he'd had since we'd arrived was catching up to him.

"You know, Stirling, I'm actually single at the moment," he began in a voice that I recognized, and one that instantly braced me into an even more heightened state of alertness. "And I miss having your massive cock inside me."

I blushed and looked around. He didn't even have the decency to lower his voice. Thankfully, no one was returning my gaze with a mortified expression, so I assumed no one had heard what he'd said.

I looked back down and spotted his arm tracing it's way across the table, like a snake that had spotted its prey.

"And since I'm only in town for another night, I thought maybe we could..."

His fingers reached my hand and I pulled it away sharply.

His eyes flared up and he let out a soft growl. This was not a man who took no very well.

"Oh, you want to play hard to get, do you? That's fine...actually that's more than fine. That's fuckin' hot."

I looked down and shook my head. I was disappointed in him, but I was more upset with myself. That I had let him creep back in through the tiniest little peephole I still had open for him for some stupid fucking reason. Well, that peephole was now well and truly shut. Permanently.

Before I could tell him that this was a mistake and that I was leaving, I felt his hand grab me roughly around my neck. I looked up and he was leaning in, looking like he wanted to kiss me...

"What the fuck are you doing?"

I shoved him off me and he fell back hard into his chair. Every single head in the restaurant turned toward us. But I didn't care. The world should see him for who he was.

"You're a greedy, cheating, lying asshole," I said, standing up and throwing my napkin down on my plate, my voice booming in the now entirely silent restaurant.

I walked away and stopped. I should have just kept on

walking out of there with whatever remaining dignity I still had. But fuck it, I had never done anything crazy or irrational in my life before...so why not start now?

"Oh and one more thing, Richard," I said, turning around to face him. "You have a really small dick."

A shocked gasp and a few giggles filled the air. Not my finest moment, but damn if it didn't feel like the best thing in the world.

I strode out of the restaurant with the biggest shit-eating smile on my face. Richard's expression was priceless. Why hadn't I stood up to him like that years ago?

I felt amazing. Seeing Richard over dinner reminded me that I actually hadn't been happy with him. Or maybe it was because I was with someone who did make me happy. Really, truly, *all the way down to my soul*, happy.

I couldn't wait to tell Mikey all about it. I could just picture his face, his eyes lighting up before bursting out into that sweet laughter of his I loved so much. And sure, the dick joke was probably more of a Nick move than a me move, but I had a feeling he would have approved.

I chuckled to myself as I took my phone out and dialed his number, pressing it to my ear as I opened the door of my truck. Hopping in, I got his voicemail but decided not to leave a message. I'd call him later and speak to him then.

The thought of hearing his voice made me smile, and that smile stayed plastered on my face the entire drive home.

For two days and two nights, I tried calling and texting Mikey. No answer.

I'd called all the hospitals and the police stations. Nothing.

I had no idea what was happening. He had just vanished. Disappeared into thin air. This was not like him at all.

I'd called Steel so many times, and he kept trying to reassure me, telling me that there had to be some logical explanation for it. His battery had died or he'd lost his phone, but I knew that wasn't it. I could feel it in my gut.

Something was wrong. Something was very, *very* wrong. I was at my wit's end.

Mikey hadn't missed a single text from me...ever. Sure, there were times when he wouldn't get back to me straight away. I never expected him to. I wasn't texting or calling him to check up on him, I was doing it because I liked feeling connected to him.

But now all there was was a whole lot of big, fat, silent nothing. For two fucking days and nights.

I tapped my fingers on the steering wheel. I'd just finished a small job, some cabinetry for a small florist. It was still early, the sun just beginning to set, casting a bright orange hue across the sky.

I looked into the rearview mirror and saw my eyes, the dark circles underneath them more pronounced than ever. I'd barely slept a wink the last two nights, worried sick about Mikey. What if something had happened to him? What if he was hurt, or kidnapped, or had been abducted by fucking aliens?

I'd had enough. I turned the ignition and sped off, the tires screeching against the road, heading for Mikey's apartment. It was a short drive to his place. I shouldn't have listened to Steel when he said Mikey would get in touch with me when he could. I knew he meant well, and there was a good chance I was going to look like a crazy boyfriend showing up in the state I was in, but I should have done this straight away.

I spotted Nick walking down the street as I pulled up. I quickly parked the truck and raced out.

"Nick," I yelled as I approached. "Nick, wait up."

I ran up behind him as he turned around to face me. His long brown hair was pulled up into a bun at the top of his head and he was wearing a faded green tank top emblazoned with *Sass & Ass*, exposing his hairy midriff and round belly.

"Mikey," I said catching my breath. "What's happened to Mikey? I haven't seen or heard from him in days."

Nick chewed his gum slowly, his whole jawline moving with each chew, as he looked me up and down. He was all attitude as he slid his bright yellow sunglasses slowly down his nose to look at me.

"I'm sorry, I don't believe I placed an order for a bucket of dicks, so fuck off, Stirling," he said as he gave me the finger and turned around to continue walking.

"Hey," I yelled, running up to him, placing my hand on his shoulder.

"Don't you fucking touch me," he said angrily as he spun around to face me. He ripped his sunglasses off his face, his brown eyes dark and raging. "You think you're so fucking good, don't you? You and your Daddy friends, think you rule Daylesford, huh?"

"Nick, what the hell are you talking about?" He was really starting to piss me off. "I just want to know where Mikey is."

Nick stepped in, standing so close to me I could smell the flavor of the gum he was chewing. It was strawberry.

"Mikey doesn't want to see you ever again, Stirling."

It was a good thing he was Mikey's best friend, otherwise the guy would have been on the ground right about now.

"I need to talk to Mikey," I growled at him.

He may have only come up to my shoulders, but Nick was one stubborn fucker.

"No, you need to turn around and fuck right off to your secret boyfriend or husband or whoever the fuck it was that you were having dinner with the other night."

Huh?

Secret boyfriend?

Husband?

Dinner...?

Damn it, Richard.

"Wait, how do you know about that?"

"Unbelievable," Nick said, shaking his head as he stepped away from me. "You're not even denying it."

"It's not what you think," I said, suddenly feeling sick to my stomach.

Somehow, Mikey must have seen me having dinner with Richard, put two and two together and gotten five.

"Right," Nick snorted. "And so says every scumbug cheating liar when they've been caught. You know what really sucks?" He stepped up to me again, putting his finger in my face. "Mikey actually thought you were different. You have no idea what you've done to him."

And with that, he turned around and walked into the building, leaving me alone on the street, surrounded by the lingering scent of strawberry gum.

I scrubbed my hands across my stubbled face, a furious fire raging inside of me. Damnit. Even though I was relieved to know that Mikey was safe, I was furious that I couldn't talk to him, that he wouldn't let me tell him my side of the story.

Whatever happened to the promise he'd made that he'd always come to me and we'd talk about whatever was going on? Was this how it would end? Without us even talking about it? With the message being delivered by Nick?

My shoulders sagged as I turned around and made my way back to my truck. Maybe dating a younger guy wasn't all it was cracked up to be.

CHAPTER TWENTY

STIRLING

"How long's it been?" Steel asked, throwing away the last of the containers from our takeout.

"A week," I grumbled as I stared out the floor-to-ceiling windows of his penthouse.

Building lights were sparkling in the night sky, and the buzz of city life hummed below us. The world kept spinning as if nothing were wrong.

But everything was wrong, at least in my world.

I dragged my hand over my chin, the stubble coarse against my fingers. I hadn't shaved. I hadn't eaten. I hadn't slept since Mikey had started ignoring me.

"Want a soda?" Steel's voice rang out from the kitchen.

"Nah, I'm good, thanks."

I took one last look at the city and turned around. Steel's apartment was almost as impressive as the view outside.

It was all exposed gray brick, sleek wood surfaces, and

shining metallic accents. All very modern. Very stylish. Very Steel. Right down to the gray monochrome colors that matched his silver locks. A coincidence I'm sure, since no one could be *that* particular. I eyed Steel in his expensively casual white hooded sweater, gray track pants, and bare feet. Hmm, well except for maybe one person.

Despite its jetsetter slickness, the place did have a warmth to it. Steel had peppered it with nice, soft touches, like the deep cushiony sofa that was calling out my name as I plonked my tired, sorry ass down on it.

Steel padded over from the kitchen and sat down at the other end of the massive sofa, a good four feet still between us.

"So what are you going to do?"

His light blue eyes lasered in on me as he brought his bare feet up onto the sofa, hugging his knees into his chest.

"What do you mean *what am I going to do?* There's nothing I can do. Mikey's the one ignoring me," I reminded him.

Not that he needed reminding. I'd been calling him every day, growing more and more out-of-my-mind crazy about this whole damn thing. And I was pretty sure I'd spent most of the evening so far rehashing everything, just for good measure.

"I don't know," I said, dragging my fingers through my hair. "Maybe this whole dating-a-younger-guy thing..."

"Don't you dare even go there," Steel interrupted. His voice rumbled thick and low.

I turned to look at him.

"This isn't about Mikey being younger," he said.

"It isn't?"

"It isn't," he said decisively, in that tone I'd heard countless times in the courtroom.

I slunk back farther away from him into my corner on the couch, creating even more space between us. I had a feeling I wouldn't like what was coming next.

"Sure, maybe Mikey could have handled things a little bit better, but..."

"But what?" I asked, although I didn't really want to know.

"But what have you done, Stirling? It's been over a week, and apart from sending him texts that he doesn't answer, and moaning and whining to me about it, what have you actually done?"

"I...uh...well..."

"What *should* you have done?" he continued, driving the point home. "What would a *Daddy* do?"

I bit down hard on my tongue. He had a point. A very good, clear, bright-as-the-sun point that somehow, in the fog of feeling sorry for myself, I had completely missed. Fuck. I scratched the back of my neck, digging my fingernails into my skin, the pain a punishment for being so stupid.

And weak.

This whole time with Mikey, I hadn't been able to open up to him the way he had to me. And now that he was gone, it hurt more than ever. Part of me felt that if I had opened myself up to him, he wouldn't be ignoring me like this.

He could sense that I was holding something back from him, so when he saw me having dinner with Richard, he'd assumed that was the secret, the thing I was holding back.

Even though he was wrong about that, he was right to not trust me. I mean, how could you trust someone when you didn't even know them? And for the millionth time in my life, not being open about who I was or what I wanted was preventing me from getting it. When was I going to learn that fucking lesson once and for all?

"If you want to be with Mikey, you have to go for it, which means, you have to go and get him back," Steel added.

Another good point.

I did want Mikey. I missed Mikey...so much. I hated not

having him in my life. I missed his constant chatter and sweet laughter. I missed his body in my bed, snuggled in tight and close to me. I missed making him feel safe and warm and...loved.

My life was empty without him.

I didn't want to go back to the life I had been living before we met. Being with him had made me see how unhappy and lonely I had been. It wasn't really living anyway, it was barely surviving. Work, court, stress, repeat. On loop, for years.

Nothing else.

No fun.

No enjoyment.

No release.

Until Mikey.

He brought all those things into my life, and so much more.

Until now.

I gritted my teeth, an anger rising within me, that I had been such an idiot about this whole thing. I had to get him back. One way or another, I had to do everything within my power to talk to him. To sit down and really, truly talk to him. About everything. Then, he could make up his own mind. But he needed to have the full picture.

I was so lost in my thoughts that I hadn't noticed Steel getting up. I only noticed when he was coming back with a file in one hand and a beer in the other.

"What's that?" I asked, looking at the thick pile of paperwork he was holding.

"This arrived in the office this morning. I've only started to look at it, but it seems to be a whole bunch of documents and emails." His eyes met mine, a glimmer of hope in them. "*Missing* documents and emails."

My eyes shot open and I lowered myself onto the floor, inspecting the papers he had laid out on the glass and metal coffee table.

"Who sent them?" I asked.

"Don't know," he said, gently thumbing through them. "Look, it might be a whole lot of nothing, or it could be..."

"Something." The hope jumped out of my mouth before I could catch it and rein it in.

"Maybe." Steel's eyes settled on mine. "Let's not get our hopes up yet."

I nodded. This court case had been dragging on for so long, and was proving to be so hard, that I didn't want to let myself get my hopes up only to have them crushed.

Because crushed hope sucks balls. Big time.

"I'll have a good look over them with the team and I'll keep you posted," he said as he pushed the file away.

"Thanks, " I said. "I appreciate it, Steel. You have no idea how much I appreciate all the work you and your team are doing. I really do. I wouldn't be able to get through this without you. The legal fees alone would bury me with anyone else."

"Yeah, well, that's what they're probably counting on. But we won't let them beat us. I will fight for you, Stirling, and I won't stop until we've won. For her," he said.

The thought of my mother filled me with even more sadness. I still missed her, but especially now. She would have known just what to say or do to make me feel better. I may have been almost forty, but sometimes, I still needed my mom.

Steel tapped his fingers on the glass-topped table as his gaze narrowed in on me.

"Yeah?" I said, not needing him to say anything. I could tell he had something on his mind.

"It's nothing, forget it," he said, waving his hand in the air dismissively.

"What? Tell me," I insisted.

"So when you um...when you saw Nick the other day outside

of Mikey's apartment," Steel began, clearing his throat, "what did he seem like?"

"Uh, he was pissed off, Steel. He was royally pissed at me," I said, sitting back on the sofa again.

"Did he seem like, I don't know, anything...else?"

He was fidgeting with the papers on the table, his normally calm, completely put-together exterior fraying ever so slightly around the edges. Subtle, but not unnoticeable.

I scrunched up my nose.

"What are you asking me, Steel?"

"Well, uh...he didn't say anything about me by any chance, did he?"

Steel's face was tense with curiosity.

In all this time I had been wrapped up in my own stuff, I'd forgotten about Steel's crush on Nick. If that's what it was...wait, was that what it was?

"You've been awfully mysterious when it comes to that boy, Steel Crawford," I said, stretching my legs out in front of me. "You haven't spoken to me or any of the guys about him. What's going on there?"

He looked down, then around the room, and finally out the massive windows, seemingly desperate to avoid what I thought was a relatively simple question.

With a deep sigh, he turned to look at me and said, "Nothing. Nothing is going on with me and Nick."

The words were prickled with hurt.

I was concerned about him. Normally, he talked. Maybe not in as much explicit—and completely unnecessary—detail as Porter did, but Steel would usually tell us what was going on in his love life. For some reason though, not this time.

"There's not much to tell," Steel said, raising his beer halfway up to his mouth, and holding it there, suspended in midair. "He didn't want to give me his number, but he took mine. And I haven't heard from the guy since."

He shrugged and took a swig.

"Oh," I said. What else could I say?

Steel usually didn't have any problems when it came to guys fawning all over him. He was a catch. Smart. Funny. Ridiculously attractive. A lawyer, but not a jerk. Well off, but kind. If anything, his problem was usually getting too much attention. Hudson and Porter had said that half of the boys at Revolver were practically throwing themselves at Steel's feet, which I was inclined to believe.

This was a whole new problem. One I don't think he'd ever encountered before.

"Do you like him?" I asked, point blank.

He nodded, taking another sip of beer.

I let the silence linger for a moment before asking him one very simple, yet familiar question. "So what have you done about it?"

"Hey, don't you get smart with me, buddy," he said, swinging his beer in my direction.

"I mean," I continued, grazing my chin in mock-consideration, "what should you do? What would a *Daddy* do?"

He grabbed the pillow off the couch and flung it at me. Quick reflexes kicked in and I clasped the pillow between my palms.

"Nice try, old man," I said. "But you don't get a pass on this. Neither of us do."

"I know, you're right," he said, nodding his head as he mulled things over in his head. "Want a soda?" he asked, standing up.

I nodded.

"Sure, thanks."

The words echoed in my head too. *What would a Daddy do?* I didn't have the answer figured out just yet, but I did know I wanted Mikey back. I did know that I wanted to be the Daddy he needed.

He had been hurt by what he saw, or what he thought he saw.

I needed to see him.

I needed to tell him what had really happened that night.

I needed to step the fuck up, clean this mess up, and be the Daddy I knew I could be.

CHAPTER TWENTY-ONE

MIKEY

"Come on, it'll be fun." Those words had become Nick's catchphrase over the last week, but no matter how hard he tried, nothing made me feel better.

We went to the movies. It didn't make me feel any better.

We went shopping, and despite having a few giggles as Nick tried on ridiculous outfit after ridiculous outfit, it still didn't make me feel better.

We even went out and got insanely drunk after Nick had finished dancing at The Tank Top. Not surprisingly, the next day, it didn't make me feel any better. It made me feel a whole fucking lot worse, with a killer hangover to boot.

We'd just gone out for lunch. Not even the crazy-good carby goodness of a Betty's burger could cheer me up. Yep, things were that bad. Once we finished our meal, we headed back to my place. I had a butler shift coming up that night, and Nick was back at The Tank Top, so we were going to get ready together. Then, Nick would drop me off to work.

"Oh shit," Nick said, suddenly stopping in his tracks.

When I turned to him, his face was screwed up like he'd just eaten a Warheads candy.

"I don't know what it is about you, Mikey," he said as his face returned to normal, "but your apartment building seems to be a magnet for asshole Daddies."

My stomach churned as I followed Nick's eyes. There, standing outside my apartment, was Brian. Staring right at us. We weren't even able to turn around, he'd spotted us. It was too late to do anything. Run, hide, scream. I reached out for Nick's arm but he had shot off, bolting down toward him.

"Nick, what are you doing?" I yelled, sprinting after him.

"Ah, the fatty and the slut," Brian spat coldly as we approached, stopping a few cautious feet away from him.

"What the fuck are you doing here?" Nick had a fury in his voice that made Brian stand up a little taller.

"It's a free country last time I checked," he said, his British accent sounding more pompously grating than ever.

I looked at the man. He was unsteady on his feet. He was drunk...again. At least he'd made it to the afternoon this time. His long black hair was neatly combed as always, his black, beady eyes hopping between Nick and me, his thin lips pursed.

"What do you want then?" Nick said the words through clenched teeth.

My heart was racing in my chest. I felt sick, nauseous. Not only had he threatened me with the video, but on top of that, I'd lost Stirling. I was *up to my teeth* sick of it. I was sick of men that treated me so badly. I felt like I wanted to scream, right there and then, on the street in broad daylight, as loud as I could.

Why the fuck was he here again? Was it not enough that

he'd ruined my life, did he want front row seats to see the shitshow play out in real time?

"Well I don't want to talk to you, fatty, that's for sure," I heard Brian say, his words slurring together.

I didn't know what happened, but hearing him insult Nick like that snapped something within me. An anger erupted inside of me, like fireworks going off. I gave Nick a gentle shove as I stepped in, inches away from Brian's cruel face.

"Mikey, what are you doing?" Nick asked.

I was doing something I should have done earlier. Years earlier. All the way back in eighth fucking grade.

I was standing up to a bully.

"Don't you ever call him that again," I said to Brian, staring him in the face and pointing my finger toward him. "If you've got something to say, you say it to me."

My finger was shaking, my whole body was, but not out of fear. I was enraged.

Being this close to him, I could smell the thick stench of alcohol on him. He lifted his head and opened and closed his mouth a few times. His eyes were glazed and his head was rocking unsteadily. Every time he closed his mouth, his lips formed into that ugly, vicious, cruel smirk of his.

What had I ever seen in him? Why had I given so much of myself to him? I shuddered at my own sheer stupidity.

"You think you're so fucking good, don't you?" he finally said. "You and your loser Daddies, trying to make my life hell."

I bit down hard.

"You're the one trying to make my life hell, Brian," I reminded him. "You started this. I'm just trying to protect myself."

I could feel Nick's breath on the back of my neck. His presence was reassuring, but I knew I had to keep going. This was my battle to fight...on my own.

"You can't fuck me over and get away with it, you little slut. No one gets to treat me like that."

I scoffed. Who the hell did this guy think he was? He was the king of treating people like crap—not just me, even his own friends, his family who didn't want to have anything to do with him, and his employees hated him, only putting up with his bullshit for a paycheck. This was the guy lecturing me about treating people like shit?

"You're pathetic, Brian," I said, and as I looked at the man, studying his face more closely than I had in a long time, the anger and the rage I felt toward him strangely started to fade away.

As long as I was angry at him, he won. Every time I gave him the reaction that he wanted from me, he won. But there was one thing I'd learned a long time ago. What bullies feared more than anything else was not being able to get a reaction from their targets.

The reactions were what they lived for, why they did what they did.

And Brian was never, ever going to get a reaction out of me again.

"You're pathetic," I repeated. "So if you want to release the video, Brian, go ahead. The whole world can see that I pleasured myself because my Daddy wanted me to. Because my Daddy asked me to make him a video that he said would be private. I'm not ashamed of what I did. My only regret is that I did it for you and not..."

I stopped myself before Stirling's name came out of my mouth.

"You don't even deserve to be called a Daddy. You're scum, you're weak, and you prey on boys so that you can feel better about yourself. But I am *done* with you."

And with that, I took one step back and one final look at the person standing in front of me.

"Let's go, Nick," I said calmly, as we walked past Brian and into the building.

As I shut the door behind us, I leaned back into it and let out a massive cry. I wasn't sure if it was a happy cry or a relieved cry, but it felt...amazing.

"What the fuck was that?" Nick asked, leaning against the door beside me. "And where did it come from? Are you Mikey Harrison? Was that really my best friend back there that did that?"

I laughed. A few tears fell out of my eyes, but then they stopped all on their own.

"I don't know what that was, Nick," I said. "I just felt...I don't know...all these years, since back in school, you've protected me. And I've always felt so bad about it, so weak..."

"Aw, Mikey—" Nick started to say.

"No, let me finish." I had to say it. "I didn't want to feel weak anymore. And I was standing there, right in front of him, looking at him, you know? This guy that I had put so much trust into, so much misguided trust, and I felt so angry. But then suddenly, the anger stopped. It just vanished."

"Vanished?" Nick asked quietly.

"Yeah, I realized I wasn't angry anymore. It wasn't about him, or Stirling, or anyone else. It was about me. I was sick and tired of feeling...ashamed. Ashamed for being who I was, liking what I liked, and doing what I did. You know?"

Nick nodded slightly and I could see him considering everything I was saying.

I saw my elderly next-door neighbour, Mrs. Gauthier, decked out in head-to-toe fluorescent pink and green sweats, approaching the door, going out for her daily walk. She was eighty-two years young and one hundred percent focused on staying fit and healthy. She smiled as she saw us both.

"Hello dears," she said as I held the door open for her.

"Hey, Mrs. G. You're rocking the sweatbands," Nick said as she flashed him a smile.

"He's always cheeky, this one," she said as she lifted a finger and looked at me.

"He is, Mrs. Gauthier. Have a safe walk," I said, closing the door behind her. "You have no idea how cheeky he can be."

Nick giggled as we walked to my apartment.

Once inside, we both kicked off our shoes and flopped onto the couch.

"That was intense, man," Nick said after a few moments, tying his hair back. "Are you okay?"

I nodded.

"Yeah, I am," I replied. "I actually am. It felt good to stand up to him, you know?"

I could see Nick rocking his head in agreement.

"I don't care about the video anymore. If he wants to prove how much of an asshole he is, he can release it. I did what I did. I can't go back and change it, but I can change feeling like shit about it."

"And what about Stirling?" Nick asked.

"What about him? It's...done."

Saying the words out loud felt weird, an awful type of weird. I had been playing every last detail of our every conversation we'd ever had in my head, over and over again. But his words were hollow, full of lies.

He'd never hurt me.

He'd protect me.

He'd keep me safe.

It was all bullshit. And I was the idiot who believed him. Correction—who *used* to believe him.

As much as I didn't want it to be over, as much as I really hoped that it was some sort of misunderstanding, as much as I wanted to give him my full and complete trust, I had to find a way to let it go.

There was no future for Stirling Bishop and me. And somehow, I was going to have to get used to that. I also had to get ready for work. I was starting in a few hours.

"Let's get ready, yeah?" I said to Nick, who looked like he had more to say.

But in all honesty, I didn't want to hear it. My mind was made up.

Things with Stirling were over...and there was nothing in the world that was going to change that.

CHAPTER TWENTY-TWO

MIKEY

It felt kinda strange going to a job without Nick.

Not that we always worked together, but since this job was at Hideaway Bay Marina, I couldn't help but think back to our last job there. It had been Hudson's birthday party and it was the night I ran into Stirling again.

The night he'd saved me from a gust of wind.

The night he'd asked me out.

Nick had been there for all of it, my rock, my protector as always. And now, I was here again but on my own. A breeze rose from the water and I shivered as I made my way to the same yacht as last time, the ironically named Lucky Boy.

When I got to the yacht, Hunter was there waiting for me.

"What are you doing here?" I asked.

He normally only helped out on big jobs or whenever we were short staffed, and from what he'd said on the phone about this job, this was a one-person gig.

"Well that's a lovely way to greet your boss," he said with a warm smile as I stepped onto the yacht.

"Sorry," I said, wincing at my thoughtlessness. "I didn't mean it like that."

"I know, it's all good. It is a small job here tonight," he said, confirming what I already knew.

He stood a little closer to me, his face suddenly drawn and serious.

"And I want you to know, Mikey, that I will be here all night, okay? If you need anything, I'm right here."

"Uh, sure, thanks boss," I said, before adding cheekily, "but I'm pretty sure I'll be fine. I might need you to rub some oil on my ass though."

His face broke out into a familiar smile.

I got changed quickly and decided to bypass the body oil. I mean, it was only a small gig. If needed, I could make sure they never saw my pale white butt. Besides, it would have been weird having my boss rub oil on my ass.

I went back to Hunter, who was ready to meet me at the bottom of the stairs to the upper deck. He was holding two glasses of champagne for me to take up.

I groaned to myself. Great, this was a romantic dinner for two. I was going to be serving some loved-up couple for the evening. This wasn't going to make me feel any more shitty than I already was.

"Those for me?" I said, eyeing off the drinks.

"For you to take up, yes," Hunter said, doing his best to hold back a grin as he handed me the drinks.

"Hey, Mikey," he said, grabbing me gently on my shoulder. "I get it now. The Second Chance Bay thing you said last time."

"Oh shit, I'm sorry," I said, feeling like an idiot. An idiot who had insulted his boss. "Nick told me about it just before we started and that's why I blurted it out. I'm sorry, I didn't mean to offend you."

"Hey, no offence taken, Mikey," he said, his eyebrows pressed tightly together. His expression was changing so quickly I couldn't keep up with it. One moment he was smiling, almost as if he were excited about something, then the next he would become super serious and look at me like I was about to be taken in for surgery or something.

"Are you okay, Hunter?" I asked. "You seem a little...weird tonight."

"What? No, I'm fine," he said a little too quickly, scratching the back of his neck as a look of guilt washed across his face. "Now go up there and...just be yourself, okay?"

"Uh, okay, sure," I said, turning to walk up the stairs.

"Oh and, Mikey..." I looked back over my shoulder at Hunter. The seriousness had returned to his face, his lips were tight and pensive. "Just remember...Second Chance Bay."

Oh god, now the poor man was talking in riddles. I tried to keep my face neutral as I nodded, but I would be back down in ten minutes to check up on him and make sure he was still speaking English.

Trying to brush that—whatever *that* was—aside as I made my way up the stairs, I prepared myself for the lovesick spectacle I was going to be witnessing for the whole night.

I felt a heaviness in my chest. I missed Stirling, I really did. Whoever said time makes things better was an idiot. The longer I went without seeing Stirling, the worse I felt. So take that, random eighteenth-century poet...I'm assuming.

Part of me felt bad for ignoring all of Stirling's texts and calls. I mean, maybe I should have given him a chance to explain. But no, I saw what I saw. He had lied. He wasn't at home fixing his leaky whatever, he was at a super fancy restaurant when apparently he didn't like super fancy restaurants, with some weird hand-holding-and-leaning-in-for-a-kiss guy.

How could he even talk his way out of that one?

I reached the top of the stairs, took a deep breath, and fixed a wide, *I'm totally fine, there's nothing to see here* smile on my face.

Hmm...that was strange. There wasn't any music playing, not even anything softly in the background. The same fairy lights as last time were up, but the whole top deck of the yacht was completely empty except for one table right in the middle of the floor. One candle-lit table. Oh brother, this was going to be next-level sickly sweet romantic. It was taking everything I had not to throw up in my own mouth.

Hmm...no music and...no people. I looked around and there really was no one there. It was deserted. That was really weird. For a second, I felt like I was about to have all my friends jump out from behind the furniture and yell, "Surprise!"

But I quickly reminded myself this wasn't my party and there weren't going to be any surprises here tonight.

I took a few steps forward before noticing a figure standing at the end of the deck. It was dark, but I could see the outline of a man. He was turned away from me, looking out over the yachts in the marina. His shoulders were broad and he wore a thick black jacket.

I took a few more steps toward him.

"Hello?" I said, realizing how nervous my voice sounded.

"Don't drop the drinks."

The man spoke without turning around. His voice was low and husky, a familiar low and husky.

"What—what do you mean?" I asked as he turned around, and right on cue, I dropped both drinks, the glass smashing onto the deck.

"Stirling, what are you doing here?" I cried.

"Don't move, Mikey, there's glass everywhere," he said as his eyes surveyed the extent of the damage, giving him the perfect excuse to ignore my question.

But he did have a point. I looked down and there was a sea of tiny shards of glass all around me.

"Is everything alright?" I heard Hunter's voice behind me. "I heard something smashing..."

"We're fine," Stirling started.

"*I'm* fine," I interrupted, looking over my shoulder at Hunter. "But I would like to know what the fuck is going on."

"I can explain," Hunter began.

"No, let me." Stirling's voice was firm, insistent. "Please."

He looked at me with those two piercing, pleading green eyes. Since I couldn't move anywhere anyway, I might as well hear the guy out.

"Fine," I said, channeling my inner Nick, and hoping it came out just as attitude-y as I had intended.

"Are you okay, Mikey?" Hunter asked behind me.

"I'll deal with you later, Mr. Second Chance Bay," I said, my eyes glued to Stirling's. "But yes, I'm fine for now, thanks."

"Alright, well I'm just downstairs. Yell, or break more glassware if you need anything."

I heard his footsteps fade away into the distance.

It was just me, Stirling, and a shitload of broken glass all around us. But in a way it was good. He couldn't come any closer to me, and whether I liked it or not, I couldn't move anywhere either.

"Here, have this," he said as he threw me a black robe.

I caught it and put it on quickly. I guess it was nice that he wasn't making me stand almost naked in front of him. But what was he doing? What was his plan here?

"I owe you an apology," Stirling said.

He looked like he wanted to move closer to me, but then remembered all of the glass around us. His face was tired, more drawn out than normal and I felt a pang of guilt in my chest. I knew it wasn't cool to completely ignore him the way I had been.

"For cheating on me?" I asked.

The words were all Nick, but the attitude was quickly falling by the wayside. I couldn't help it. Standing here, even if it was a few feet away from him, I felt drawn toward him. It was stronger than ever, despite everything.

"I didn't cheat on you, Mikey," he said in a low grumble as he took a step forward.

The glass crunched underneath his shoe. He looked down for a second, but then continued walking, crunching his way closer one slow, deliberate step at a time.

When he reached me, my heart was in my chest. The salty night air mingled with his warm, earthy scent and it sent prickles of heat across my skin. He reached his arm out.

"No, don't touch me," I said as I wrapped the robe tighter around myself and looked away from him. I wasn't ready to feel his touch. It was hard enough just being this close to the man.

"I won't," he said, bringing his hands back toward his body and taking a crunch-filled step back away from me as well.

"What you saw that night was me having dinner with Richard."

"Your ex?" I asked, looking up at him.

The expression on his face was full of pure, gut-wrenching pain. He nodded.

"I'm sorry that I had dinner with him. I regretted it the instant I sat down at the table with him. And I'm sorry I didn't tell you about it, but you were at work, so I was going to tell you afterward. I swear I was. I even called you as I was leaving the restaurant because I totally made a scene."

"You? Stirling Bishop, you made a scene?"

Who was this man?

"Richard is a dick. He tried to hold my hand, but I pulled away. Then he leaned in for a kiss and that's when I lost it."

My heart stopped beating. That was what I had seen at the restaurant—and that was the exact moment when I looked away. I was so sure that I was about to see that man kiss Stirling that I couldn't bear to watch.

"What—what happened next?" I asked apprehensively.

"Well, that was when I made a scene."

His lips were pushed upward in the faintest hint of a smile, but I could tell he was a little embarrassed too. He wasn't the kinda guy that *made scenes*.

"I got up and yelled at him in front of the whole restaurant," Stirling said as a gentle blush filled his cheeks.

"I'm impressed."

My heart resuscitated itself and began to make its way from my throat back into my chest.

"There's more."

"More?" I asked, my eyes widening in disbelief.

No, seriously, who was this man standing in front of me?

"Yeah, as I was leaving I turned around and I announced to the whole restaurant that Richard had a very small dick."

"You did?!" I burst out laughing. "That's so funny."

"I'm not proud of it, but I thought you'd like it," he said as the seriousness returned to his face. "I'm so sorry for all of this, Mikey. I never meant to hurt you. I would never do that on purpose."

His words hit me hard in the chest. I took a moment, I probably took a few moments actually, letting it all sink in.

Stirling was a good man, I knew that. I could trust him. I wanted to trust him. I believed him.

Finally, I spoke.

"I'm sorry too. I shouldn't have ignored you. I should have

come to you and talked to you about what I saw...the way I said I
would. But I didn't. I'm so sorry, Stirling."

My words mingled with the salty breeze. The silence that
fell between us was the comfortable kind, the type that felt close
and real and so, so fucking good.

"Can I touch you now?" he asked.

I hadn't even finished nodding when I heard a crunch and
felt Stirling's warm body pressed against mine. I sank deep into
his towering chest as his strong arms encased me softly. It felt so
good to be wrapped up in him again.

When he pulled away from me, I missed his touch straight
away. I didn't want to miss his touch anymore.

"Would you like to join me for dinner?" he said as the sparkle
returned to his eyes and he flashed me his dazzling smile.

"Uh, yeah, sure," I said, my head was still spinning from all of
this. "Should I go get it? I am technically the butler here tonight."

"It's all taken care of. I ordered some Betty's burgers and
fries. Hope that's okay?"

"What about a—" I began.

"And a strawberry milkshake too," he said as he snuggled me
into his chest. "As if I could forget that."

CHAPTER TWENTY-THREE

STIRLING

It felt incredible to be sitting across the table looking at Mikey's beautiful face lit up by candlelight. No, scratch that, it felt fan-fucking-tastic.

I couldn't believe how close I had come to letting him slip away. I had been moping like an idiot for the better part of two weeks, when a simple conversation was all that was needed.

I apologized to Mikey because I wanted to, because it was the right thing to do. But I had to admit it also felt good to hear him apologize to me as well. Being shut out like that hurt so badly, but the feelings I had for him gave me the strength to pull through and step up.

Whatever last remaining sliver of doubt I had about him being immature because he was younger was well and truly gone. He owned up to what he did and I believed him when he said that he wouldn't do it again.

Finding a way to see him had been no easy feat. I figured

since he wasn't taking my calls and he kept ignoring my texts, I had to find another way to reach him. With the help of Hunter, and Nick—yes his overprotective, bundle-of-sass-and-attitude best friend, Nick—I was able to pull this evening off.

Explaining things to Nick wasn't easy, but after he tired himself out with his finger wagging, side-eye death stares, and sassy one liners, and actually let me explain, he turned out to be really supportive of this plan. I could see why he and Mikey were best friends. He was protective, loyal, and only had Mikey's best interest at heart.

Speaking of best friends, Steel's words had motivated me to get off my sorry ass and actually do something about this situation. Steel was right, I had to step up and be a real, proper Daddy. The Daddy I knew I had in me. I needed to get out of my own way, and let my inner Daddy come out and do his thing.

Funny thing was, it was a whole lot easier than I thought it would be. I had gotten myself so caught up on words like *Daddy* and *boy*, that I'd forgotten that it wasn't about labels, it was about people. It was about people being real and honest and talking with one another.

I knew what I had to do. Porter's stupid three-point plan laid it out so plain and simple that even a knucklehead like me could get it. I knew what I wanted, I'd figured that part out. Now I just had to step up and say it, and hopefully, *hopefully*, if Mikey was into it too, we could go for it.

Mikey was devouring that burger like I wanted to be devouring him. He caught me looking at him, because he immediately stopped chewing and reached for a napkin.

'What?" he said, covering his mouth.

"Nothing," I said, smiling. "I just like looking at you."

"You're thinking," he said as he put the napkin down. "I can always tell when you're thinking."

He was right. I had been thinking about a lot of things over the past few weeks. But in amongst it all, there was one thing I'd been thinking *a lot* about.

Mikey had told me about his desire, his need to please. The more I considered it, the more my respect grew for him. There was something so awe-inspiring in the strength and trust that was needed for that sort of...submission.

Because ultimately, that's what it was. It was a form of submission. He would be letting me be in control and take charge. His pleasure would be inexorably woven into mine.

And in return, I would take care of and protect him from everything. Especially from asshole ex-boyfriends that had misused and abused this beautiful boy's trust. I would never let that happen to him again. No one would ever hurt Mikey like that.

"So," I said, swallowing down hard around the lump forming in my throat. "You've asked me a question a few times about what I'm into, and I believe I still owe you an answer."

His eyes flared with heat as he adjusted himself in his seat.

"I've never told anyone this before," I began as I took a deep breath.

"It's okay," Mikey interrupted. "You don't have to tell me anything if you're not ready. I—I can wait, Stirling."

There was a reassuring comfort in his voice.

I shook my head and unclenched my jaw.

"No," I said firmly. As much as I appreciated the kindness in his offer to wait, I didn't want to wait anymore. "I want to tell you. You deserve to know."

And so I did. I told him. *Everything.*

How I didn't have it all figured out in my head just yet. How I loved the thought of lightly spanking him, but never in a degrading or humiliating way. How I loved the sound, the feel, the look of it. How I had never done anything like this before, but that I wanted to try and that I wanted to try...with him.

The more I spoke, the more my heartbeat slowed and I eased into an almost effortless flow of conversation. For the first time, it felt like my mind and my mouth were working as one. There was no delay, I was able to say exactly what I was thinking.

When I finished speaking, I let out a deep breath and smiled at Mikey. He was staring at me with a burning fierceness in his eyes. His expression nothing but pure, unadulterated lust.

"And now," I said with a relieved smile washing over me, "I believe it's your turn to say something."

"Nice, I see what you did there."

His voice was laced with humor and...understanding. He looked out across the bay, taking his time, before turning to look at me. My eyes were transfixed on the boy sitting across the table, examining every last detail of his smooth boyish face, impatiently waiting for his reaction to what I had said.

I cleared my throat, hoping it would hurry him a little. I wasn't normally impatient or pushy like this, but I had just shared the most private, intimate thing about myself to him. It was the most vulnerable I had ever felt in front of someone. I could feel my heart pounding against my chest again as I was hit with the enormity of my words, and the chance that he could react badly to them.

I mean, I had no idea if he was even into spanking. While he had told me what he was into, he'd been vague on the specifics. *Within reasonable limits* could have meant a thousand different things. I needed him to say something. Why wasn't he saying anything?

"Yeah, that's cool. I could get into spanking, if that's what you want," he said with a casual shrug. "Have you got a safeword in mind, or can I come up with my own? And have you thought about what position you'd like me in while you spank me? And what about spanking equipment? Would you like to just use your hands, or would you prefer a paddle, or something else?"

Safeword.

Position.

Equipment.

"Uhhh..." It was all I could manage.

"That's right," Mikey said, flashing that cheeky, adorable smile of his. "I forgot you're a first-time Daddy. I guess we can just take our time and figure this out... together?"

I nodded my agreement.

I looked out across the bay, at the yachts gently swaying with the breeze as they bobbed in the water. I felt a warm rush of relief flood through me. For the first time in years, I finally felt at peace.

"Have you guys finished your meal?" Hunter asked gingerly, stepping onto the deck.

"We have, yes, thank you," I replied.

Hunter quickly scooped up the plates and cleared the table. "Would you guys like dessert now or would you like to wait a while?"

"Oh, I've got dessert covered," Mikey said, quirking an eyebrow.

Our eyes locked together. A lust blazed in me, wild, fierce, and unrelenting. I could tell Mikey was feeling the same.

"Alright then," Hunter said, reading the room and he swiftly disappeared.

As soon as he was out of view, Mikey pounced up out of his chair and strode over to me. He sat down in my lap and whispered into my ear, "I think I'd like to go back to your place."

His words went straight to my cock, which hardened on the double. I was sure he could feel it pressing up against his thigh. Mikey shuffled himself in my lap, the friction feeling so good against my rock-hard length.

"Sometimes, we don't need words," he said, breathing seductively into my ear. "Sometimes, all we need is two bodies, two thick, rigid cocks, and one strong Daddy spanking his boy."

That was all I needed to hear. I got to my feet, scooping Mikey up. He wrapped his arms around my neck as I strode across the deck of the yacht.

"You want this?" I asked him as the fairy lights danced across his boyish face.

"I do...Daddy. Let's go back to your place."

"Oh, my beautiful boy. I've missed you so much. I...I love you, Mikey."

"I love you too, Stirling."

His eyes were so full of love when he looked at me it made me weak in the knees. I tightened my grip around him and took my boy home.

It was done, it was finally all out in the open. I had opened up and told Mikey what I wanted. What I really, truly wanted. I had revealed something to him that I hadn't shared with anyone else in the world.

There were no more secrets between us. We had both revealed ourselves—our truest, rawest selves to each other. And I was going home to make love to the boy I loved.

It felt incredible.

No scratch that, it felt out of this world fan-fucking-tastic.

CHAPTER TWENTY-FOUR

STIRLING

I didn't remember saying goodbye to Hunter as Mikey and I left the yacht.

I didn't remember getting into my truck and driving us back to my house.

I didn't remember anything until we walked through my front door, and Mikey launched himself into my arms, showering me with deep, urgent kisses. The sweet taste of him filled my mouth and unleashed an insatiable hunger within me.

A delightful sensation of happiness blossomed in my chest and spread through my entire body. I was leaving everything behind. The old me, that wouldn't talk, that wouldn't say what he wanted, that wouldn't *go* for what he wanted.

He was gone, replaced by this man. The man I'd always wanted to be. The protective, strong Daddy looking out for his boy, with his boy pleasing him in return.

With Mikey straddling me, his legs wrapped around my

waist, I carried him into my bedroom. He didn't make it easy for me though, the naughty boy, kissing me with such a powerful greediness that I stumbled more than once, unable to see where I was going. Thankfully, I somehow managed to avoid furniture and walls and we made it into my room and onto my bed in one piece.

I tore the robe off Mikey and untied the small apron around his waist. His naked body lay out on the bed before me.

"Do you have any idea how beautiful you are?" I asked him, surprising myself when I realized that I could even talk.

The sight of him was beyond breathtaking.

"Uh, yeah," he said, cocking his head to the side and unleashing that gorgeous, cheeky smile of his. "I'm a fucking catch."

I laughed and nodded my head in agreement. "That you are, Mikey boy. You are a catch...and I've caught you. You're all mine."

The cheesy words felt good coming out of my mouth, and by the way his cock twitched, I could see he liked it too. I traced the my fingertips across his entire body, from his collarbone, down his smooth, slender torso to the tops of his thighs. I could feel the quivers of pleasure rippling through him underneath my fingertips.

I was taking my time deliberately, partly because I was enjoying having Mikey back in my bed. I wanted to relish every precious second as I remembered all the tender spots on his body that responded so beautifully to my touch.

Another part of me though was enjoying the anticipation. I knew what was coming. I knew that Mikey would let me spank him. The thought of that turned me on in a way I had never experienced before.

I wanted to enjoy that feeling, the joyful apprehension of the pleasure to unfold. Pleasure I would experience for the first time ever with Mikey.

My boy.

My sweet, sweet boy.

Mikey, on the other hand, wasn't in the mood to be patient or go slow. He was ready. He tore off my pants, grabbed my rock-hard cock, and gave it a few tugs, spreading the precum down my shaft. The wetness underneath his fingers, sliding across the sensitive skin of my cock, felt incredible.

This boy had some seriously talented hands. Whether they were rubbing my feet or gliding up and down my cock, his touch created the most unbelievable sensations that tore through my entire body. There was no way I could resist him.

He turned around, positioning himself on all fours right near the edge of the bed. He wiggled his tight, pert ass at me.

Looking over his shoulder, his eyelids heavy with lust, he whispered, "Fuck me, Daddy."

I swallowed down hard. He wasn't going to have to ask me twice. I stood up and walked to the end of the bed, my hard and heavy cock bouncing out in front of me. I lubed my cock up until it was glistening with grease. He wiggled down some more, so that the tip of my cock was perfectly positioned, pressed against his eager, ready hole.

I felt his ass twitch, as if he were telling me how hungry he was for me. Not one to wait for his Daddy to take control, Mikey shoved himself back against me, taking me inside of him. His tightness encased the first few inches of me and it sent a jolt of heat up my spine.

I blinked hard and readjusted my feet, needing to steady myself as Mikey's willing body was on a clear mission: to draw me in closer.

I grabbed him around his hips and took half a step toward him, thrusting my full length into him. He arched his back and let out a sweet moan as his head kicked back. The sight of him bucking as he took my cock made me even harder inside of him.

I gave him a moment to adjust, but he didn't want to stop or slow down. He started grinding against me, pushing back onto my cock. *He* was fucking *me* and it was the most beautiful thing I'd ever seen. My boy was needy, pushy, and hungry...for me.

"Spank me, Daddy."

His breathless words filled the room and with all the strength I had in me, I plunged my cock even deeper into him. My heart was racing out of control.

This was it.

This was the moment I had been waiting for, yearning for, fantasizing about my whole life. Right here in front of me with this beautiful, *beautiful* boy, giving it to me. Giving me exactly what I wanted.

"Are you sure?"

"Yes, yes..." he panted breathlessly.

"I don't want to hurt you."

"You won't, you won't."

He was riding my cock intensely now. My breath hitched in my throat. The thrill of what was happening was building up at the base of my spine.

"Just do it. Spank me, Stirling!"

Mikey's words were a command, a command I had to obey.

I raised my hand and smacked him lightly across his right cheek. The sound of the crisp slap filled my ears and drove me even farther into him. Mikey arched his back in response. I increased the rhythm, thrusting into him harder and with even more force.

"Ahhh, I like that, Daddy," he said, barely able to get the words out, his head and whole body rocking against my body. "Can you give me one more smack...please?"

I thought I was going to lose my mind as I slapped his left

cheek, harder this time. I looked down and could see his skin flushed, the faintest outline of my hand still painted on his ass.

I drove into him, harder and faster. His body meeting every thrust with abandon, he was giving as good as he was getting.

"I love you, Mikey," I panted.

"I love you too, Stirling," he said breathlessly, his body rocking underneath me. He turned over his shoulder and yelled out, "One more smack, please, Daddy!"

I thought I was going to lose my mind, overdosing on the sheer ecstasy of it all.

I raised my hand up into the air...

MIKEY

...Stirling's heavy palm smacked across my ass cheek with a filthy-sounding slap. The initial sting quickly gave way to the most incredible burst of pleasure I'd ever felt. Well, since the last slap anyway.

The heat it produced spread across my entire back, inflaming my skin with a deep red flush, as Stirling—*my big, strong Daddy*—continued to thrust into me from behind. His pace was building, his long, hard strokes filling me up and satisfying me in a way I'd never experienced.

I hadn't ever been spanked before, but from the moment Stirling had mentioned it on the yacht, I knew I was in. All in. There was no way this man would ever hurt me or get off on degrading or humiliating me in any way. I knew that and I trusted him. Completely.

What he had shared was his fantasy, something that he wanted to try...with me. I could tell how hard it was for him to tell me. Hell, I'd been waiting for months for him to finally open up to me. And he finally did. And it had been worth waiting for.

There was no better feeling in the world than being free like this. With Stirling's heavy balls slapping against me with every forceful thrust, I knew I was pleasing my Daddy. I felt safe with him. Safe to lose all of my inhibitions and with a pure, reckless abandon, give myself, all of myself, to him.

To his wants and needs.

To the things he wanted to try with me.

To his pleasure.

I knew he would never judge me or hold anything against me.

My body was hungry, needy. I needed to please him. I needed him inside of me. I needed to turn around and see that weird, contorted look he got on his face whenever he was close to exploding.

I needed it more than anything else. To submit and to please was part of who I was, and knowing that he knew that, accepted that and loved me for it, was beyond anything I ever thought possible.

I could feel his balls tightening. He was getting close. So was I.

He threw his body weight down on me and started nibbling on my ear, the sensation flushing my body with heat. I lost my grip and fell down, collapsing onto the bed with Stirling's strong, sweaty body on top of me.

He was heavy, but a good kind of heavy.

His thick fingers slid around my throat, my head rocking wildly as he continued to pound me with his enormous cock. The friction of his fingers around my neck felt incredible. He was squeezing gently, not wanting to hurt me, just letting me know he was there. Oh fuck, I knew he was there.

He was on top of me.

He was inside of me.

He was everywhere I wanted him to be.

His teeth released and he gently licked my earlobe, making me buckle.

"Mine," Stirling groaned in that low rumble of his that made my heart instantly pound against my chest.

"What?" I gasped with what little energy I had remaining in me.

"Mine," he repeated, his hips thrusting harder, more forcefully against my body. "You're all mine."

And with those words, we both reached the edge and came at the same time, our sweat-covered bodies thrashing into each other. His guttural groan into the back of my head met my deafening screams.

The force of our shared orgasm bound our bodies together, shaking, spasming, twisting, until finally...*finally*...the sensation began to subside.

The sounds of breathless panting filled the room, both of us trying to catch our breath. Stirling slowly pulled out of me. The instant he was gone, he pulled up beside me on the bed and guided me into his body, cuddling me possessively.

He grabbed a pillow and gently placed it under my head. With the pads of his fingers, he delicately traced over my flushed cheeks as I nestled into the soft pillow.

I was filled with the warm afterglow of sex and about a gallon of Stirling's cum inside of me. I guess the man hadn't blown in a long time. That thought brought a smile to my face, as I shuffled back, pressing into him harder, feeling his release inside of me.

"Did you mean it?" I asked after a few moments.

"Mean what?" Stirling's voice was deep and unguarded. His chest beating furiously against my back the only sign that he was coming off the same massive high that I was.

"That I'm...yours?"

"Yes," he said as he interlaced his fingers around my middle, pulling me in even more snugly. I could already feel his cock start to thicken against me.

I beamed as I lay there, with his strong body around mine.

I was his.

All his.

CHAPTER TWENTY-FIVE

MIKEY

"You're doing good," I said encouragingly as Nick staggered behind me. The massive present he was holding in his arms was slipping further and further out of his grip and sliding down his body as we made our way to Porter's front door. "Just a few more feet. Come on, you can do it."

"Remind me again why I'm doing this," he puffed as he stopped for a second, rocked the present back up his body, and tried, unsuccessfully, to clasp his hands together around it at the front.

I smiled. He didn't even come close, the thing was way too big. And way too heavy.

"Uh, because you're my best friend and I've done tons of crazy shit for you, so you owe me one million favors."

"That sounds about right," he grumbled as we reached the thick, wood-paneled front door. He leaned against the wall and let out a massive sigh. "This fucker is heavy."

"Well, we're almost there, so stop complaining and follow me in."

"Just so you know," he said as I opened the door and he picked up the present again, "I am dropping this in the entry as soon as I get in."

And that he did. He walked through the door, took a few steps to his left, and lowered the present to the floor.

"Thanks buddy," I said, pulling him in and messing up his hair. "You're the best."

"And now you, my friend, owe me a drink," he said with a friendly pinch to my arm.

"I can get you both a drink."

Nick and I turned around and saw Steel standing there with a hopeful smile on his face. His thin white cashmere sweater hugged his body tight, as if it were painted onto his muscular torso, shoulders, and arms. It contrasted nicely with his tanned skin and brought out his distinctive light blue eyes.

"I'm good, thanks, Steel," I said as I loosened my grip on Nick and moved away slightly. "But my friend here has worked up a bit of a thirst."

"Uh, no, I'm good too, thanks," Nick said, uncharacteristically quietly as he leaned in behind me, almost as if he were using me as a shield.

"Oh, okay then," Steel said a little dejectedly. "The birthday boy is over in the corner, by the way."

"What is your problem with that guy?" I whispered as soon as Steel had walked away from us.

"What?" Nick grumbled defensively. "I can get my own damn drink."

And with those surly words, he sulked over to the open bar.

Shrugging my shoulders, I made my way over to the corner and to the man of the hour. The birthday boy. My boyfriend.

His face lit up as he saw me approach. He was standing in

the corner with Hudson and Porter, the three men huddled in nice and close, as if they were deep in conversation.

"The party can stop right now," Stirling said as he wrapped his hands around my waist and pulled me in for a kiss, "because my present just arrived."

"Oh no," I said, pulling back a little and placing my index finger against his lips. "Your birthday present is coming later...*Daddy.*"

I heard an, "Oooh," come from Hudson and Porter's direction. There weren't many people around us, but I didn't care. I didn't care if the whole world knew he was my Daddy. I would have shouted it from the rooftops and let all of Daylesford know if I could.

I was madly in love with Stirling Bishop.

And I knew, beyond a shadow of a doubt, that Stirling Bishop was in love with me too.

It was good to see him happy and smiling with his friends. He'd been doing a whole lot more smiling in the last week, ever since he and Steel had won that motherfucker of a court case.

Apparently, someone handed in a whole bunch of evidence to Steel's office. Evidence which ended up proving to be invaluable. It showed emails and records of phone calls where the facility had failed to act to help Stirling's mom.

It was a bittersweet victory for Stirling. On the one hand, it didn't change anything. His mom was still gone, taken way too early over something so stupid, so easily preventable.

But on the other hand, he got a very handsome settlement out of it. One that would set him up for the rest of his life and at least go some of the way toward compensating him for all of the stress and anguish he had been put through over the last three years.

It was like a massive weight had been lifted off his shoulders. He was happier, lighter than I had ever seen him. And he was sleeping better than ever. I mean, maybe I had something to do with that. Our bodies did snuggle in and fit so right against each other as we drifted off to sleep together almost every night.

"It's so good to see you guys together," Porter said as he walked up to us. "I don't expect to get a thanks out of you, Mr. Bishop, but I know Mikey is a lot more well-mannered and gracious than you are."

"What am I going to be well-mannered and gracious about?" I asked as I sceptically looked over at Porter.

I could see Stirling rolling his eyes and shaking his head next to him.

"Oh brother, here we go again," he said as he drew me in close to him.

"Wait, what?" Porter said with mock surprise. "You haven't told Mikey about my patented three-point plan?"

"Three-point what now?" I asked Porter.

He launched into some incredibly long story about some patented plan he had devised for Stirling and I to get together. I smiled as I listened to him. This was obviously some joke between friends that I was not in on.

He had finished talking and was staring at me with an expectant look in his light green eyes.

"Thanks," I said with a wide grin. "We uh...we owe you one."

"Just have wildly amazing sex, that's all the thanks I need," he said, grabbing us both by the hand and giving a squeeze.

"We will," Stirling rumbled in his deep, low voice. "But let me assure you, Porter, you will be the last thing on my mind when we do."

We all laughed as Nick and Steel approached us. Had they been talking? Had they finally worked through whatever weirdness they were going through? Could they just hurry up and get together already?

Before I could pepper them with any of the questions racing

through my mind, I saw Steel lugging my incredibly large and heavy present for Stirling across to us.

"I found a helper," Nick said, shooting me an evil, self-satisfied smirk.

He walked up next to me and folded his arms across his chest as we watched Steel stumbling his way over to us, barely able to keep himself upright, the present practically tipping him over.

"Steel, that's so heavy. You shouldn't be carrying it by yourself," I said when he got closer.

"Oh, but it was okay for me?" Nick asked, turning to me with an unimpressed look on his face.

Hudson, the gentle giant, walked over and took it from a very relieved Steel. He was able to wrap his arms around it, making it look like he was carrying a grocery bag, not the awkward, bulky thing I had ordered from Morocco. He placed it on the floor near Stirling.

"You owe me one, remember?" I shot back to Nick. "Hey, listen, guys, since you're all here, I just want to thank you. You've been so amazing in helping me with..."

I so didn't want to even say his name again.

"Your ex?" Hudson offered delicately, straightening himself out.

I nodded.

"Yeah, thank you. I know how much you've all done."

"Hey," Steel said as he walked over to me and placed his hand on my shoulder. "Stirling's our brother. We'd do anything for him. We're all family here. Which means, you're family now too."

"Guys, stop it. I'm getting teary over here," Porter said, pretending to dab his eyes and wipe away the tears.

"You'd have to have a heart to get emotional," Hudson added

and we all laughed. "But, I am curious to see what the fuck is in that heavy box"

"Well, I wanted to get you something special," I said, turning to Stirling. "Something that's a reminder about how we met, and something you wouldn't forget."

"I don't think my lower back is going to forget about it anytime soon," Steel mumbled under his breath, but loud enough for us all to hear.

I saw Nick chuckle for a brief moment, before catching himself and drawing his expression blank again. Something must have really been up between him and Steel if he wouldn't even allow himself to laugh at the man's jokes.

Stirling knelt down and eyed the heavy package on the floor.

"Can I open it?" he asked, looking up at me with those piercing green eyes. They were alive with excitement.

"Of course," I said with an enthusiastic nod.

To my surprise, he didn't take his time. I thought he'd be one of those people that opened a present delicately, as if they were trying to save the wrapping paper for another gift. My ma may or may not have been one of *those* people.

But no, the usually calm, steady, slow, meticulous Stirling was like an excited kid opening up his presents at Christmas. He flung his arms around in an over-the-top, animated way as he tore the wrapping paper off the present. When it was finally uncovered, the gift stood there, unwrapped in front of all of us.

"Oh wow..."

"Is that a...?"

I could hear the guys' voices in the background, but my eyes were locked on Stirling. My heart started beating faster as I searched his face for signs of a response.

After what felt like an eternity of silence, I finally asked, "Do you like it?"

Stirling stood up and strode over to me, his heavy hands

framing my face as he pulled me in for a long, deep, passionate kiss.

"I guess that answers that question," Porter said, lifting his hand to his lips and speaking through the side of his mouth to his friends. I heard a round of low chuckles.

"I love it. Thank you," Stirling said.

A searing heat throbbed under my skin as he kept his gaze fixed on me.

Seeing him so happy ignited parts of me I never knew existed. Whether it was giving him a present he liked, or pleasing him in the bedroom—or in the kitchen, or on the sofa, or in the back of his pickup truck at the bird sanctuary in the middle of the night—there was no better feeling in the world than knowing I was pleasing, serving, my Daddy.

The man who looked after me and made me feel safe and protected. Even though I felt more confident that I could look after myself now and didn't *need* his protection, it felt incredible knowing it was there anyway.

"Uh, you guys," Nick spoke up and we all turned to look at him.

In typical Nick fashion, he paused for dramatic effect, soaking up every last drop of the attention we were giving him.

"What the fuck is it?" he eventually asked, pointing at the unwrapped gift sitting on the floor in front of us. His face was crinkled in confusion.

We all laughed.

"Don't you know?" I asked, shaking my head. How could he not see what it was?

"Uh, no," he said sheepishly as his cheeks turned a hot red.

"It's a footstool," Stirling explained, trying to suppress the smile on his face.

"Oh, now I get it," Nick said, nodding as it all finally made sense to him. "I see what you did there."

"What?" I replied all wide-eyed and innocent. "I just thought it would look good in Stirling's living room."

Porter lifted his hand to cover his mouth and tilted his head as he whispered sotto voce to the group, "Had nothing to do with you getting tired of being Stirling's personal footstool, did it?"

We all laughed at his joke.

"I could never get tired of being Stirling's personal anything," I said as he pulled me in for an impromptu, yet heartfelt hug. The warmth between our bodies sizzled.

I looked up at him, into those shimmering green eyes of his, those eyes I could stare into forever.

"But I can think of some naughty things we could do on that footstool," I whispered as I leaned in close so that only he could hear.

"Oh yeah, like what, Mikey boy?" he whispered back, his voice so deep it sent a shiver down my spine.

"Well, maybe you could strip me down, bend me over it and then...*spank me?*"

"Guys, great party but we gotta go!"

And with that, Stirling picked me up in his arms and carried me out of Porter's house, my body rocking joyously against his as we walked down the moonlit driveway.

"Oh no," I said with a giggle, bouncing in his arms as we walked toward the street.

"What is it baby?"

"We left the footstool inside."

He let out a low grunt.

"Doesn't matter. I might ask Porter to deliver it. There's no way I want to break my back lifting that thing."

"That's right," I said as I tightened my grip around him.

My boyfriend.

My man.

My Daddy.

"I can think of much better ways to break your back."

"Oh yeah?" he asked.

A smile stretched out across his lips, as if they were inviting me to lean in and kiss them. So I did. Pressing myself into his soft, fleshy lips, a soft moan escaped from me...or wait, was it from him?

How did I get so lucky? Having this big, strong, burly man carrying me and making the softest, sweetest-sounding moans at the same time?

"Have you had a good birthday?" I asked when we got to his truck and he gently lowered me to the ground.

He stepped in, the moonlight shining off the edges of his face and hair, illuminating his handsomeness in a translucent glow.

"I got the best present in the world."

"I'm glad you liked the footstool," I teased.

"I wasn't talking about the footstool," he said with a seductive smirk.

"Well then what are you..."

"You," he whispered. His voice deep and husky, his eyes dancing across my face. "All mine."

I didn't need a man with a lot of words. Just a few perfect words were fine with me. I smiled, my heart overflowing with love.

My Daddy had found his voice.

And I'd finally found my Daddy.

I was his.

All his.

EPILOGUE

FIVE YEARS later

STIRLING

"Everyone's staring at us," I said, as we made our way, hand-in-hand, slowly down the corridor.

"That's because you've got a fine ass," she said.

"Or maybe it's because you're holding my ass?" I said with a chuckle as I lifted her arm, which had *accidentally* slipped, and placed it back around my waist. For the third time.

"That's better," I said.

"Is it?" came the reply.

"Now look, Mrs..."

Her head snapped so fast I was sure I heard it crack.

"Sorry, I mean, Mom...I mean, Ma."

"That's better," she said with a satisfied huff. "Now, I am listening to you."

"Let's get you back to your room, alright? The specialist should be in to see you any minute now."

As we approached the door to her room, she turned to look at me. Her eyes softened as she spoke.

"Thank you, Stirling. Thank you so much for everything."

"You don't have to keep thanking me...Ma," I said. "I'm just so happy that you're here, getting the treatment you need and being looked after so well."

"You're a good man, Stirling," she said as she drew me in for a gentle hug.

"I'll see you later, okay?" I said.

She nodded as she made her way into the room.

"I need to see that fine ass at least twice a day. The doctor says it's the best type of therapy for me."

"Sure, sure," I said with a smile, making sure she got to her bed safely before turning to leave.

I was happy that she was getting the treatment she needed.

Her condition had deteriorated quite quickly in the first year after her diagnosis, sending Mikey and Ben out of their minds with worry. But thankfully, over the last four years, the doctors had found the right combination of drugs and lifestyle adjustments to see the rate of deterioration stabilize and slow down substantially.

And I was genuinely happy that she was here, getting the best level of care possible.

I hadn't known what I wanted to do with the money I won in the settlement. I hadn't fought the case for money. It was never about that for me. I'd just wanted justice for my mom and I'd wanted to make sure that no one else had to go through what I went through. Seeing the people responsible held to account for what they did was all the victory I had hoped for.

I certainly wasn't expecting a fifteen-million-dollar settlement. After compensating Steel and his team handsomely for all of their hard work and dedication over the three brutal years the court case had dragged on for, I knew what I wanted to do with the rest of the money.

So I did it.

I bought a nice big parcel of land on the outskirts of Daylesford and built an aged care facility. No amount of money would ever bring mom back, but at least the Barbara Bishop Aged Care Facility would live on and be her lasting legacy. My small tribute to her.

It also meant that Mikey's mom had a place where she could be looked after. Properly. All the patients here had top-notch care. This place wasn't about making a ton of money. It was always about people first, not profit. Everyone here was treated with the dignity and respect they deserved. No one would suffer the way my mom had. No one.

I stepped into my office and walked over to my favorite part, the photo wall. The sheer joy and bliss in those photos was more than I could have ever expected in my life.

And of course, Mikey was in pretty much all of the photos, because it was pretty much all due to him that my life was as wonderful as it was.

I smiled as I looked over our wedding photos. He'd finally gotten me into a suit, the only time in five years he'd succeeded in doing that. I didn't scrub up too badly, I had to admit, but it was my boy in a suit that really took my breath away.

Even now, looking at the photo three years later, made my heart flutter. His beaming smile, the beautiful view of the mountain range behind us, the reception we'd had at the restaurant in the bird sanctuary. From our first date there to our wedding, that was by far my favorite place in the entire world.

Then there was the photo from our beach vacation, *before* Mikey got stung by a jellyfish and broke out in a rash that prevented me from taking any more photos of him on that trip.

Or the photo of the two of us at the bottom of the Eiffel Tower in Paris, with Mikey's face covered in chocolate. I had no idea Mikey was afraid of heights until halfway up the rickety elevator to the top when his face started going pale and he looked like he was going to faint.

I didn't get to propose to him at the top like I had planned, but I managed to do it at the bottom instead, at a cute cafe by the river, while he stuffed his face with a chocolate croissant.

All the wonderful, joyous memories came rushing back in a heartbeat. That was why I loved this wall, it took me back to the happiest moments of my life every day. The best thing about it was that the wall wasn't even close to being fully covered, so we had plenty more time to keep making more of those precious memories.

All because I had met a boy who did something to me that no one had ever been able to before: he got me to open up and talk. To say what I wanted. I felt safe with him, knowing that I could tell him anything, no matter how hard or uncomfortable, and we would be able to deal with it. Together.

I sighed as I looked over at the mountain of paperwork sitting on my desk, but I wasn't quite ready to quit my daydreaming just yet.

MIKEY

"Knock, knock," I said as I stepped into Stirling's big corner office.

His face lit up in surprise. Seeing Stirling happy never got old.

"Hey, you," he said. He was standing by the photos on the wall. I swear, the amount of times I'd walked in and seen him standing there, looking at them, I had to wonder if the man ever did any work at his desk. He walked over to me.

"I thought you were working today?"

I leaned into his warm embrace, letting his strong arms wrap themselves around me.

"Mix up with the rosters," I explained. "I'm doing night shift instead."

"Well this is a very pleasant, unexpected surprise," Stirling said, eyeing the footstool in the corner of his office with a devilish grin.

We may or may not have bought footstools for pretty much every room of our house, and for Stirling's office. It was nice, our own private thing. I mean, it just looked like a normal piece of furniture...to the untrained and unknowledgeable eye, that is. But for us, it was a constant reminder of how we met.

We may or may not have *acquainted* ourselves with each and every footstool as well.

But right now? At ten in the morning on a Thursday? In his office?

"Why do you think the door has a lock on it?" he asked, his voice a low growl, as if he were reading my mind.

"And why do you think I soundproofed this office, Mikey boy?" he added for good measure.

He stepped in toward me and dragged his fingers through my now auburn, mid-length hair. Black hair was like, so five years ago.

"Well, don't you have the appetite today, Daddy? You already fucked and spanked me, before we even got out of bed this morning," I said, heat pooling in my belly.

"What can I say? My husband is irresistible. I'm weak to his powers."

Hearing my big strong man telling me I made him weak at the knees made me rock hard.

"As much as I'd love to, we can't," I said, stepping away from him, giving him a knowing look.

I didn't trust that I wouldn't be flung over the footstool and getting my ass slapped into a nice shade of light rose-red if I didn't move away from him. I could feel the need pouring out of him.

"Oh, is she outside?" he asked.

"She is," I said. "I couldn't get her past the reception staff. You know how much she loves to talk to everyone."

I rolled my eyes.

"Yes, she definitely likes to talk...to everyone."

I walked over to the photo wall.

"I really wish you would take this down," I said, pointing at the only non-photo on the wall.

"Why?" Stirling said, walking up behind me and throwing his arms over my shoulders. "It's my favorite."

"You say that about everything on this wall," I said as he nestled his face into the crook of my shoulder.

"A man's allowed to have more than one favorite, isn't he?"

God, I loved it when he spoke like that. So innocent-sounding and yet, so raw.

"It's not even a photo," I protested.

"It's not, but it means something to me," he said as he walked over to the graduation certificate. "The University of Daylesford has conferred onto Mikey Harrison the qualification of Registered Nurse."

"It's embarrassing," I moaned.

"Hey, no it's not," Stirling said, his face stiffening. "I am so proud of you, Mikey. You worked hard for it. You failed your childcare entrance exam three times before switching over to try nursing. You failed that entrance exam twice before you finally got accepted."

"That's what's embarrassing," I said.

"No," he corrected me. "That's why I'm so proud of you. You didn't give up. I don't know anyone else who would have tried as many times as you did. But you. That's one of the reasons why I love you so much, Mikey boy."

I guess Ma was right. Things happen when the time is right. I didn't see it back then, in fact, I hated the whole experience of trying and failing to get accepted somewhere. But now, I was so glad I'd persevered.

I finally had a job, a proper job. One that helped people and made a real difference in their lives, including my mom's. Working as a nurse at the facility meant that I could look after her and keep an eye on her to ensure she was doing everything she was meant to do.

Besides, it's not as if I could have been a naked butler for the rest of my life. What people say about metabolism slowing down as you get older is so true. I was only just approaching thirty and already I had gained, like, twenty pounds. Okay, more like five, but still...

"Should we go out to her?" Stirling asked with a twinkle in his eye.

"Yes, we need to save your reception staff. She's probably talking their heads off."

"I'm sure they don't mind one little bit," Stirling said as he interlaced his fingers with mine.

We strode down the hallway, hand in hand, reaching the reception to see everyone huddled around her. Stirling was right, they were fussing and cooing over her like they'd never seen a baby before.

"How's my beautiful little girl?" Stirling asked as he lifted her high up into the sky.

She let out a series of delighted giggles.

May Bishop, our beautiful ten-month-old daughter, loved to

be swung around, and she loved her Daddy and her Papa more than anything else. It had taken us a few attempts, and the journey was hard, but seeing our daughter happily laughing in Stirling's arms made it all worthwhile.

Her name was Stirling's mom's middle name, and since she was born in the month of May, it all fit perfectly.

Stirling brought her down into his chest as I leaned in and gave her a kiss on her soft forehead. She looked up at us, blinking those wide, bright blue-green eyes that made both of us melt. She opened her mouth, giggling, and began to excitedly wave her arms around, while Stirling pulled all sorts of cutesy faces at her.

She was such a happy, good-natured baby, and standing there with her in the safety of Stirling's arms, and his love for her so evident, I'd never felt more at peace in my life. I had found a man that I could trust and who I knew would never hurt me. Or our baby girl.

I didn't think it was possible to be any happier than I was at that moment.

I was wrong.

Two syllables proved me wrong.

With Stirling continuing to make all sorts of ridiculous googly faces at her, she stopped giggling and waving her arms around. Her eyes went from me to Stirling and back to me again, and then...

"Da-da."

The two syllables ricocheted in my head. I turned to Stirling, who looked at me at the same time. He was beaming. Our baby girl had just spoken her first word. It was the most beautiful sound I had ever heard.

I squeezed his arm as I could see the corner of his eye mist up.

We looked down at our May, smiling, looking up at us. Not

knowing all the joy and love she brought to our lives. My heart couldn't handle any more happiness.

As we both looked down at her, she looked at both of us and said it again.

"Da-da."

THE END